On the Other Side of the Cul-de-Sac

On the Other Side of the Cul-de-Sac

Miz B

CONTENTS

Copyright © 2025 by Miz B
All rights reserved. No part of this book may be reproduced in any manner whatsoever without written permission except in the case of brief quotations embodied in critical articles and reviews.
First Printing, 2025

PROLOGUE
TEDDY & MONICA

Crickets.

That's the only thing that could be heard on the ride home. Eight-year old Lil Teddy sat in the backseat gleaming about his softball team's victory and their celebratory pizza party while his parents, Monica and Teddy, rode in complete silence, not wanting to argue in front of their son. The short ride from the softball field to the house seemed like a long one, but as soon as they got home, Monica instructed Lil Teddy to get in the tub to erase all the dirt off his body after all his sliding around on the ball field. She couldn't wait to tear her fangs into Teddy.

"You really think I'm stupid and blind! You think I didn't notice that you were texting that bitch, Yasmine, at the game? Every time you would send a text message, she'd look at her phone and smile. Your face would light up each time you got a text. I thought I was watching a tennis match instead of a softball game from the way you two were carrying on. I'm tired of your disrespect! I'm your wife. The mother of your son. And you treat me like I'm the crap on the bottom of your shoes!" Monica threw the cell phone at Teddy, and the screen cracked as soon as it landed on the pristine kitchen floor.

Teddy felt his blood start to boil, so he walked out of the room, but Monica was not done. Following him into the next room, she continued her rant.

"Oh, you think you can just walk away, and I'll let this go? Over and over again, I deal with your whoring ways. You promise me time and time again that you're a changed man. Do you even know how many men would appreciate a good woman like me?" She pointed her finger-nail into his back while he reached inside the drawer to pull out a fresh shirt.

Trying to keep his composure, he remained quiet, but the clench of his jaws couldn't hide the fact that he was bothered. He closed the drawer and turned around to face his irate wife, whose eyes were red from anger and pain. She glared into his and carried on with her verbal attack, but Teddy was not in the mood, so he walked into the master suite to take a shower and tune Monica out.

"I've wasted twelve years of my life dealing with your lying and controlling ways! Enough is enough, and I'm taking Lil Teddy and we're leaving!"

Teddy stopped in his tracks. The veins popped out of the side of his neck. He turned around and angrily glared at his wife.

"What did you just say?"

"You heard me. I said I'm tired of your disrespect. I'm tired of you cheating on me while I try my hardest to be a good wife to your ungrateful ass. I'm tired of wondering how many more women are out there that I don't know about. You don't deserve me! You don't deserve my son!"

"Bitch!" was all Teddy said. He grabbed Monica's neck and looked into her eyes while she struggled to breathe.

Her eyes bulged out of their sockets while she tried unsuccessfully to pry Teddy's fingers from around her neck.

"Every other day, I have to listen to your idle threats. Let this be the last time you threaten to take my son."

Before Monica blacked out, the last words she faintly heard were, "Mommy, I'm finished taking a bath."

Eric & Leila

Chapter One
ERIC & LEILA

Two years later

She opened her eyes to the sun peeking through the blinds and the birds chirping the song of a new day. Leila just knew that the day was going to be a beautiful one. She turned over and looked at her husband, Eric, who was still in a deep sleep after their long night of making love and enjoying the temporary break they had from parenthood. With their ten-year-old son, Julian, away for the night, Eric took advantage of the situation and sexed Leila in every corner of the house until they ended up spent and fully satiated in their king-sized nest.

Leila stared at her sleeping husband with love in her eyes, enjoying the sight of him. To her, their bond never got old, and each time they made love, she'd fall head over heels all over again. Even in his deep slumber, he was extra handsome with his low-cut wavy hair, his boyish face with a slight hint of a mustache that he purposely kept low, his thick smooth eyebrows, and his luscious, kissable lips. The morning sun rays were peering through the windows and highlighted his rich amber skin tone. She sighed, drinking in his manly beauty. *He's all mine*, she thought, recollecting ten years ago when she said, "I DO" and couldn't think of a time where she regretted her decision. Eric was the love of her life, and she knew the feeling was mutual.

He stirred in his sleep, and his eyes slowly crept open. When he saw Leila's sexy brown eyes staring back at him, his lips formed a smile, quickly remembering the intense lovemaking session they had last night.

"Hey sleeping beauty," Leila teased.

"Hey sweetness. What're you doing? Thinking about the way I put it down on you last night?" he asked in his deep, groggy voice.

Smirking, she replied, "If I recall correctly, we put it on each other."

"Mmmm...that we did," he agreed. "You must be ready for another round?"

The smoldering look in her eyes answered his question, but before he could roll over to follow through with his wife's silent request, she lifted the covers up over her head. He watched her covered body travel down to his middle region and proceeded to wake the sleeping giant. Eric closed his eyes once more, but not to go back to sleep, but to enjoy the wake-up call that his wife had initiated.

***

Leila's phone was blaring in her ear on the nightstand and startled her out of her sleep.

"Oh shoot! Did I fall back asleep?" Leila looked at her phone and saw that her sister, Kyndall, was calling. Her husband was lying comfortably next to her, asleep too. After their last round of pleasure, they both dozed back off, not caring about the time, the outside world or anything else.

"Hey sis," Leila answered.

"Uhm...do you know what time it is?" Kyndall responded. "Julian and I have been ringing the doorbell for way longer than we care to. What are you doing? Nevermind...I don't want to know."

"Sorry sis. Eric and I dozed back off. Here I come to the door."

Leila threw on a robe so she could let her son and her sister inside. When she got to the door, Kyndall looked her up and down with a knowing look on her face. Leila's long curly hair was a bunched-up mess atop her head, and she looked as if she'd been in a wrestling match. Ignoring Kyndall's look, Leila let them inside and greeted her son.

"Hey baby. Did you have a good time with your aunt?"

Excitedly, Julian answered, "Yes, mommy! Aunt Kyndall took me to Dave & Buster's and we had soooo much fun!"

"That's nice, baby." Leila beamed at Julian. She loved the bond he had with his aunt and knew that her sister would make a wonderful mother one day. "Go put your things up, and don't forget that you and your dad are going to the store today to pick up a birthday gift for Lil Teddy's party."

Julian ran to his room with his bag so he could tear into the new video game that his aunt bought for him until it was time to go pick up the birthday gift. Kyndall sat her purse on the table then fell back on the cushiony couch.

"You might as well get comfortable. I need to go shower and get myself together," Leila guiltily expressed to her sister.

For dramatic effect, Kyndall rolled her eyes and sighed. Her sister was never on time and they had made plans to go shopping and get mani/pedis. "Please do, because you look like you been—"

"Shhh...I already know what you're going to say. And, yes, me and my hubby had a wonderful time." Leila fluffed out her tangled curls with a huge grin on her face. "Thanks for giving us a much-needed break. Did you and Julian eat?"

"While you were sleeping and getting your back blown out, Julian and I had breakfast fit for a king and queen. Will you go shower, please? And tell my brother-in-law to get up. The day is almost over."

After Leila shooed her away and rushed back into her bedroom to shower, Kyndall inwardly laughed—she loved to tease her big sister. Throughout the years of watching how Eric treated her sister, Kyndall was dead set against settling for anything less until her king came out of hiding. Eric set the bar high for any and all potential suitors, but she had high hopes that it would happen one day—hopefully sooner than later.

She knew it would be a while before Leila got dressed, because "slow" was her middle name, so Kyndall went to the refrigerator, poured a glass of orange juice, then walked out back to the screened-in lanai to soak in the bright, spring sun. She loved the peace and tranquility of their spacious backyard. It was like stepping out into a professionally landscaped oasis at a resort, complete with a covered gazebo, a stone water fountain, top of the line patio furniture and exotic plants that created an outdoor zen den.

When Eric and Leila moved into the newly developed neighborhood months ago, she fell in love with the quiet community and all the houses nestled away in the cul-de-sac. It was the type of environment she wanted for her family when the time came; however, waiting for Mr. Right seemed like it would never happen. Being back on the dating scene after a two-year roller coaster of a relationship with Devon, she felt that the prospects were gloomy. She sighed, dismissing those thoughts, and then as if he read her mind, her phone buzzed with a text from her ex.

I was thinking of you and wanted to know if we could meet up this week for dinner

Kyndall shook her head before deleting the text. *I refuse to waste any more of my valuable time with that idiot!* Devon proved time and time again that he was unable to keep his privates private, so when the last woman approached her at the coffee shop about "her" man, Kyndall eventually decided that she no longer wanted the drama that came along with a serial cheater. She'd turned over a new leaf and refused to give anyone the time of day that didn't want the same things that she wanted. Being that she was on the verge of turning thirty-years old in a few months, she felt her biological clock ticking and refused to continue to nourish a dead situation. Kyndall wanted what her sister had—a loving man and family. They were the ultimate relationship goals, and she was determined to reach her destination.

After an hour of deleting emails, text messages and pictures of Devon, Kyndall heard Leila's voice.

"Sis! I'm ready."

Like she didn't just have Kyndall waiting over an hour, Leila stepped out onto the lanai looking bright and refreshed in a long, colorful maxi dress and thong sandals. Her curly hair was up in a bun, showing off her flawless face.

"You look cute sissy, but I am not amused," Kyndall said while getting up from the comfortable, cushioned patio chair. "Let's go so I can put these feet in some bubbly hot water."

"Yes, let's!"

Eric walked out in his pajama bottoms and a tank. Kyndall gave him a scolding look.

"Hey brother, it's your fault. I'll never make plans with Leila again."

Eric chuckled, giving Kyndall a hug. "You know your sister is always late...that'll never change. Enjoy yourselves. I'm bout to blend up this protein shake to bring me back to life. Your sister zapped all my energy."

"TMI bro...TMI," Kyndall laughed.

Leila gave Eric a kiss before the sisters walked out the front door. While walking to Leila's car, Kyndall checked the time on her phone and shook her head.

"Sis, we don't have a whole lot of time. I thought you said the party starts at five."

In her usual casual manner, Leila responded, "It does. We have enough time to get a good pedi, but we will probably have to shop another time."

Kyndall was just about to give Leila a piece of her mind when her eyes caught sight of the tall, light chocolate man jogging in their direction. Kyndall's eyes traveled from his handsome face to his muscular bare chest that was glistening with sweat down to his black jogging shorts that caused her imagination to roam. As if in a hypnotic state, she watched him in slow motion jogging towards them until he got near and slowed down. His closeness and his smile made Kyndall's heart race slightly. For all those reasons, she couldn't take her eyes off him.

"Hi, Leila," he spoke as he slowly passed by. "Hi," he said once again, looking at Kyndall with a wide smile spread across his sweaty face and a sparkle in his eye. He took notice of the pretty woman who was with Leila.

"Hi, Teddy. See you at five," Leila said, waving as Teddy slowly jogged by and unaware of her sister's sudden distraction.

Kyndall watched a little while longer then got in the passenger seat of Leila's car.

"Uhm...who was that?"

"That's Teddy."

"Is he married?"

Leila looked over at her sister who seemed to be smitten. "Yes and no. He lives on the other side of the cul-de-sac. Remember the man I told you about...his wife went missing a couple of years ago?"

Kyndall's eyes widened incredulously. "Wow! That's him?"

Leila nodded her head while backing out of the driveway.

"Yes, girl. He's a very nice man, and his son, Lil Teddy, is who's having the birthday party this evening. He plays on the same baseball team as Julian and invited a few of the players from the team to help celebrate. He's a sweet little boy. I just feel so bad that they never found his mom."

"That breaks my heart," Kyndall responded. "Is he still in mourning? Is he dating? How is he handling everything?"

Leila made a complete stop at the STOP sign and curled her lips at her sister. "Dang! Are we inquisitive. Honestly, though, I think he has something going on with one of the team moms, Yasmine. She's always giving him the eye, hanging around him like they're a couple...you know the type."

"Shoot! I can't blame her. Did you see him? He's gorgeous."

"Girl, I'm not looking. My baby, Eric, is all the man I need to look at."

"Well, we can't all be so lucky." Kyndall playfully rolled her eyes.

"Stop hatin'."

"Please! Oh, and I'm coming to the party. What should I bring?" Kyndall laughed.

Leila giggled. They continued talking while making their way to the nail salon.

The Party

CHAPTER TWO
THE PARTY

Later that evening, Lil Teddy's birthday party was underway. He was ecstatic about turning ten years old—a double-digit milestone in a kid's life—except deep down inside he wished his mother was there. Instead of dwelling on his inner feelings about his mother's disappearance, Lil Teddy was preoccupied with his teammates and a few neighborhood friends that showed up to help celebrate. He couldn't help but to have a good time with all the excited commotion going on and friends running around the blue and gold decorated backyard that was set up like a carnival with a batting cage, a water slide, and a bounce house along with a table of endless sweet treats to keep the kids on a sugar high.

"Thanks, Mom for helping decorate. You did an amazing job." Teddy stood next to his mother, Felisha, while they watched the kids run around the yard.

"Anything for my grandson." She smiled while they both watched Lil Teddy from afar running around having a good time with his friends. "He looks so happy right now...just how a kid should look."

"I try to keep him busy so he doesn't have a lot of idle time to think."

"That's all well and good Teddy, but he needs to be able to talk about his mom and express his feelings about her not being here. I don't want my grandson holding in all those feelings. Does he even try to talk about her?"

"Mom, I won't allow it. He's just a kid. He shouldn't have to deal with adult situations."

Lovingly looking into her son's eyes that matched her own, Felisha tried to give him some words of wisdom. "Monica is...was...his mother, and she was very attentive and doting. I'm sure her absence is having an effect on him, and just because he's not outwardly displaying those feelings does NOT mean they don't exist."

Feeling himself getting aggravated by the conversation, Teddy cut his mother off. "Mom, can we talk about this later? This is supposed to be a fun day. We have more guests coming," he said, pointing at Eric, Leila and Julian coming through the gate. He dismissed his mother and put on a happy face.

"Hi neighbors. Thanks for coming," he greeted them.

Eric shook his hand. "Thanks for the invite. We would've never heard the end of it if we hadn't brought Julian to the party of the century. That's all he's been talking about since Lil Teddy gave him the invitation."

Julian looked at his father like he overdid it.

"Mom, you remember Eric, Leila and their son, Julian, from the team. They live on the other side of the cul-de-sac."

"Yes," Felisha replied with a smile. "Thanks for coming. Julian, I'll put your gift right here, and you can go join the fun."

That's all Julian needed to hear. He nearly threw the gift on the table and dashed over to his other teammates who were engaged in all the fun activities. He couldn't wait to try the batting cage. The adults laughed, watching him run full speed ahead.

"I hope you don't mind, but my sister came along for the fun," Leila said to Teddy. "She's still in the car freshening up her makeup."

"Dang, Sis. You didn't have to give him all that extra information," Kyndall walked through the gate with a big smile on her face.

Teddy eyed the beautiful, light-chocolate toned woman that he'd noticed earlier during his run around the neighborhood. She was simply dressed, yet stunning, in a short blue romper with gold accessories and stylish sandals, and her long, black hair was in a high ponytail.

Smiling, Teddy replied, "No, I don't mind at all. The more the merrier. Thanks for coming, and I love the way you all color coordinated to match the theme of the party. Everyone looks great."

"Thanks, Teddy," Kyndall coyly responded.

"Help yourselves." Felisha pointed to the table. "Teddy has the good stuff in the kitchen, though," she informed, winking her eye.

"I think I'll try some of the good stuff." Kyndall said with air quotes. "How about you, sis?" She looked at Leila.

"Not right now. Eric and I will take a load off and drink some of this kiddie punch."

While Eric and Leila got some punch and joined the other parents who were seated in the lawn chairs on the other side of the yard, Kyndall followed Teddy into the kitchen that overlooked the enormous backyard. He fumbled in the cabinet for a glass, and Kyndall helped herself to a seat at the island. While he looked for the perfect glass, she admired the view of his strong back and arms in the blue t-shirt he wore.

"What would you like to drink?" he asked, turning around and pointing at all the different bottles of adult beverages he had on the island.

Kyndall quickly acted like she wasn't just in a trance, cleared her throat, and answered, "How about some of that Malibu with pineapple juice."

"Good choice." Teddy made her a drink. "So how come I've never seen you around these parts?"

"Hmm...I don't know. Maybe we crossed paths and didn't know it."

"Trust me, if we crossed paths, I'd remember."

Kyndall blushed.

"Your sister and Eric are a lovely couple. They're always so nice."

Kyndall imitated vomiting by putting her finger down her throat. "Yea, they're couple goals."

They both laughed at her gesture.

"So I take it you're not married?"

"No, but I'm crossing my fingers. Wish me luck."

"As beautiful as you are, I'm sure it'll happen for you sooner than later."

Demurely smiling. "Thank you. From your mouth to God's ears." She raised the glass he'd given her and took a sip.

She wanted to mention that she heard about his wife's disappearance but didn't want to overstep or seem like she was prying, so she let it go for the moment. However, after they got comfortable talking and she had gathered up enough liquid courage, she addressed the elephant in the room.

"Let me know if it's none of my business, but my sister told me about your wife. I just want to say, I'm sorry."

Teddy's whole body tensed up. He wasn't expecting to have that conversation with any of his guests, let alone someone he just met. His eyes shifted from being caught off guard. He took an unnoticeable deep breath to give himself time to respond like a politician.

"Thanks for your sentiment. It's been rough on me and my son, but we're continuing to hold out hope that one day she'll walk through those doors in one piece. On the other hand, with the length of time that she's been missing, I don't know if that day will ever come."

Concern spread across her face as she saw how hurtful the situation was to him.

"I'm sorry. I didn't mean to bring it up on such a celebratory day. If there's anything in my power that I can do, please let me know."

"Thanks, Kyndall. I appreciate your kindness."

***

Sitting inside the car in front of Teddy's house, Mark and his mom, Cynthia, were preparing themselves to make an entrance inside Lil Teddy's birthday party. Mark sat on the driver's side tightly clutching the steering wheel while his mom tried her best to get him in a festive mood to celebrate his nephew's birthday.

"I know it's hard for you to make nice with Big Ted, but this is not for him. We're here for my grandbaby. Lil Teddy is looking forward to us showing up, and his innocent face lights up every time he sees his Uncle Mark. I want you to get that chip off your shoulder, put a smile on your face, and make your nephew happy just by being here." She put her finger underneath his chin and commanded him to look at her.

"This is hard for me too, Son. I miss Monica just as much as you do. But we have to continue to stay positive and pray that one day, hopefully soon, that she'll be found. Lord knows I miss my daughter sooo much." Cynthia kept her strong resolve. She couldn't afford to be emotional at the moment, especially while trying to get Mark in the right frame of mind.

Mark took a deep breath. "Okay, Mama. You win. I'm doing this for Lil Teddy, but I'm letting you know now…if Big Ted looks at me wrong and let his mouth say something I don't like, I can't promise that I'll be able to contain myself."

"Enough! Let's get in here before my grandson starts to wonder if I'm going to show up. I promised him I'd be here early, and I'm sitting out here trying to talk you off the ledge. I don't want no mess, Mark. You hear me?"

"I still don't trust him, Mama. If I find out he did anything to my sister—"

"Stop! Now is not the time. This is Lil Teddy's day. Let's get inside."

Cynthia stepped out of the car with a giftbag in hand and walked towards the backyard gate with a stubborn Mark following closely behind. He loved his nephew as if he were his son, but having to endure Big Ted and his fake concern for Monica's disappearance was too much for Mark to handle. However, he promised his mom that he'd try to be on his best behavior, so he intended to keep his word.

Lil Teddy was having the time of his life running around with his teammates, but when he saw his grandmother and Uncle Mark, he dropped everything, ran to them like he was Speedy Gonzales, and fell into his grandmother's embrace.

"Gran!"

"Happy birthday, baby!" She swallowed him up in her arms and almost had a meltdown thinking about how Monica had missed another birthday. Cynthia kept it together, kissed him on the top of his head, and released him from her arms.

"How does it feel to be ten?"

"It feels great!" He animatedly spread his arms wide to exemplify how great it was, causing his grandmother to laugh.

He then approached his Uncle Mark, and they gave each other their signature handshake that they made up when he was three years old.

"Happy birthday, Nephew!" Seeing his nephew smiling and having fun on his birthday worked wonders to soften his mood.

"Thanks for coming."

"I wouldn't miss it for the world."

"Lil Teddy!" his friends screamed, waiting for him to return to the batting cage.

"Go ahead and play with your friends. Your Gran and I will be here until the end." Mark gently squeezed Lil Teddy's shoulder.

"Okay! I'll be back."

After Lil Teddy ran back to his friends, Cynthia and Felisha exchanged pleasantries. The two women were always cordial, but they were not on the same page when it came to their grown children. Felisha was known to have her nose stuck in Ted and Monica's business and taking Ted's side even when he was wrong. Cynthia, on the other hand, tried to stay neutral throughout the years and let the couple work through their own issues.

Felisha thought that Cynthia was a goody two shoes, and outside of their common bond, the two would not be friends. She had to silently admit that Cynthia was a welcomed sight when Lil Teddy's face beamed when she arrived. Since Monica's disappearance, the two women had to put aside their personal feelings and focus on their grandson's wellbeing. Their love for him somewhat bonded them together.

"Where's Big Ted?" Cynthia asked.

Pointing towards the sliding glass doors, Felisha responded, "He's inside."

Both Mark's and Cynthia's eyes followed Felisha's finger and saw Ted standing in the kitchen with a glass in his hand laughing with a female they'd never seen before.

"Oh," Cynthia simply responded. "I'll wait for him to come out." She then walked over to where the adults were congregated.

Mark wasn't so nonchalant. Witnessing his brother-in-law entertaining another woman while his sister was still missing caused his temperature to rise.

"I think I'll go say hi." Mark walked with purpose and stepped inside. His entrance interrupted Kyndall's and Ted's laughter, and they turned towards him. Kyndall's bright smile and sparkling eyes unexpectedly struck a chord. Mark felt an instant attraction after making eye contact and momentarily forgot why he stepped inside the kitchen in the first place until Ted's voice broke the spell.

"Oh, I see you made it," Teddy unenthusiastically stated.

Taking his eyes off the beautiful woman, Mark glared at Ted. "Only for my nephew."

"Kyndall, this is my bro...uh...my son's uncle, Mark."

Smiling, Kyndall reached out her hand to the extremely handsome man. "Hi Mark. Kyndall. So, you're the birthday boy's uncle?"

Taking her soft hand in his, Mark replied. "Yes, my sister, Monica, is his mom...Ted's wife."

"Oh." Kyndall didn't know how to respond to his sharp response. She could tell that there was some tension between the two men, and she wanted no parts of their family drama. She picked up her glass and headed towards the door. "Thanks for the drink, Teddy. I'll be outside with the rest of the guests. Nice to meet you, Mark."

Mark nodded his head, and the men stared each other down until Kyndall was out of earshot.

"I already knew you weren't shit, but to sit here entertaining another woman while my sister's whereabouts are still unknown, is mighty bold of you and downright disrespectful."

Teddy clenched his jaws at Mark's accusations. "Listen here, I don't owe you any explanations, and the only reason why you're even here is because MY son wanted you here! Don't get it twisted and mistake my kindness for weakness...you're the one being disrespectful by coming in MY house and flexing your muscles."

Mark balled up his fists. He wanted to jump across the kitchen island and pummel Teddy's face, but before he could get a chance to further contemplate his actions, Felisha stepped into the kitchen. From outside, she saw the tense interaction between the two, and decided to intervene before something happened.

"Remember, this is Lil Teddy's day," she reminded the men. "I think it's time to take the cake out and sing happy birthday.

Mark took a deep breath, turned around and went back outside without saying a word.

Felisha chastised her grown son. "I'm going to need for the both of you to make nice. This is not easy on any of us."

"Mom...I'm done with being nice to Monica's brother. He's always had animosity towards me, and since she's been gone, the tension has only gotten worse. The *only* reason he's allowed at my house today is because of Lil Teddy. After today, he better not step foot at my door!"

Felisha waved him off and proceeded to take the cake outside so the kids could gather and sing. When the kids saw the cake, they stopped everything and ran. They were in awe of the elaborately decorated cake that was shaped like a baseball field with plastic ball players placed on the bases and at the different positions on the field.

"Happy birthday to you, happy birthday to you, happy birthday Lil Teddy...happy birthday to youuuuuu."

They all sang, cheered, and clapped. Lil Teddy enjoyed the limelight, beaming from all the love. He leaned over, closed his eyes, and made a wish before he blew out the flaming blue and gold candles. Wishing that his mother was home, he opened his eyes and believed with all his might that his wish would come true since all ten candles were no longer lit.

3 |

The After Party

CHAPTER THREE
THE AFTER PARTY

The celebration was winding down, and the children were full, dirty, and tired. The exhausted parents were ready to get them home, bathed, and bedded.

"Do you need help cleaning up?" Leila asked.

"No, but thanks for the offer. My mom is going to stay behind and get everything put back together," Teddy advised.

"No problem. We're getting ready to take Julian home, but don't hesitate if you need anything, seriously, Teddy."

A sly grin appeared on his face. "Uh...about that...you think your sister would be willing to help for a little while?"

Leila cleared her throat and looked over at her sister who was entertaining the remaining kids and jumping inside the bounce house.

"I can't take her nowhere," Leila giggled. "I'm sure she won't mind, but let me ask."

"I promise I'll make sure she gets back to you in one piece. Scout's honor," he said, holding up his fingers.

"I trust you."

Making her way to Kyndall, Leila eyed Yasmine, the flirtatious team mom, having a conversation with Eric. She could tell by Yasmine's body language that she was trying to entice her husband. Yasmine thought that every man was putty in her hands due to her green eyes, shapely body and creamy skin tone. Leila shook her head and laughed. The stoic expression on Eric's face let her know that he was being polite but wanted to run. Through the years, she had to deal with countless women trying to push up on her husband. He definitely had his share of women trying to come on to him, but he only had eyes for his wife. They'd talk and laugh about it later; however, she figured she'd save him. She walked over and tapped him on his shoulder.

"Hey baby," she announced, ignoring Yasmine.

He turned towards her, and she put her arms around his neck, looking into his eyes with a smile on her face.

"Is everything good?" she asked. "It's time to get Julian together so we can go home."

"Yes, babe." He bent down and kissed her.

Yasmine shifted uncomfortably and flipped her hair, watching the two lovebirds.

"Nice talking to you, Yasmine." Eric walked off.

With a tight smile on her face, she waved.

"It's been fun, hasn't it?" Leila asked with a smirk. She could tell that Yasmine was uneasy.

"Yes, it has."

"See you around." Leila walked off, giggling to herself.

Yasmine walked away looking for the next victim to entice.

After playing mind games with Yasmine, Leila called Kyndall down from the bounce house and told her about Teddy's request.

"You know that he is technically still married, so...." Leila added.

"Girl, I'm not trying to marry the man. Besides, that lady been gone all this time, I don't think she's coming back, if you know what I mean."

"That's a mean thing to say."

Kyndall shrugged. "I'm not trying to be mean or insensitive...just being honest. Anyway, I'm not gonna do anything inappropriate. His son is here, and I'm just going to simply lend a hand. Nothing more. Nothing less."

"Okay, sis. I said my peace. We're about to get out of here and take Julian home."

"As soon as I'm done, I'll be back over there."

Leila gathered her husband, her son, and a few to-go plates and headed home.

Mark and Cynthia said their goodbyes to Lil Teddy. Cynthia hated the division that existed between the two families. She intended to have a sit down with Teddy, Mark, and Felisha to discuss a better way for them to be actively involved in her grandson's daily life. It was bad enough that Monica was not present, so he needed each and every one of his close family members to be on one accord and put their differences aside for the greater good.

She hugged her grandson tightly. "I love you soooo much, and don't you ever forget that. Anytime you need your Gran, I'm here, okay?"

"I know, Gran. I love you too. I'm happy you came to my party."

Cynthia held back the tears. "I wouldn't have missed it for the world. Make sure you put all your things away tonight. You got some pretty good gifts today."

Excitedly, Lil Teddy, replied. "I know! I can't wait to set up my new game!"

"Yeah, buddy!" Mark joined in. "Let me know if you need help with that, okay? And like Mom said, we're here for you anytime. I love you, nephew."

"Thanks, Uncle Mark. I love you, too. Can I come over next Saturday?"

"You sure can, but we'll have to make sure it's fine with your dad." Mark was seething on the inside knowing that Ted was going to make it difficult for him and Lil Teddy to hang out. However, he was going to put his pride aside for his nephew.

"Yah! I can't wait!"

Lil Teddy ran off after finishing his goodbyes with his grandmother and uncle. Before leaving, Mark looked through the glass door and saw Teddy in the kitchen laughing and carrying on with the pretty woman, Kyndall. Then he noticed the flirtatious team mom standing off to the side mean mugging the exchange between Teddy and Kyndall. She was unaware that anyone was watching her.

***

All the guests had left, and the house was quiet. Teddy was grateful to everyone who showed up to help his son celebrate his monumental day. He had just tucked Lil Teddy in bed, although it took some time for him to come down from his sugar high. After putting up his gifts, taking a bath and saying his prayers, the junior eventually passed out, but not before praying out loud for God to protect his mother, wherever she was, and to let her return home safely before his next birthday. Teddy was at a loss for words, so he just kissed his son on the forehead and sat on the edge of the bed until he closed his young, tired eyes.

Teddy went into the kitchen, looking around to make sure everything was tidy before he shut it down for the night. A smile spread across his face as he thought about Kyndall, his "new friend" and was truly grateful to her for sticking around and helping out with the cleanup. She left with a promise that he'd treat her to lunch or dinner to show his appreciation. He had sent his exhausted mom, Felisha, home, letting her know that she had done more than enough with decorating and setting up the party. The fact that she didn't protest was confirmation that she was drained.

His phone buzzed on the counter. It was a message from Yasmine.

I saw you making googly eyes at Julian's aunt

Shaking his head at her audacity, he sat the phone back down, not wanting to disrupt his peace and engage in angry text messages with Yasmine. He figured he'd straighten her out tomorrow; she was an easy fix and never stayed mad too long once he showed her some "special" attention. Besides, he had someone else he had to visit before he went to bed, so he began his nightly routine. He took a napkin and cut a small piece of the leftover birthday cake, then walked into his bedroom and locked the door. He retrieved the remote from his dresser drawer then stepped inside the custom built walk-in closet. After clicking the remote, the tall wall of shoes slid over, revealing a hidden door. Once he stepped inside the cavernous, secret space, he held up the piece of cake and devilishly smiled at his wife.

"You missed a good party, Monica. Our son is becoming a young man right before our eyes."

Where's Monica?

CHAPTER FOUR
WHERE'S MONICA?

2 Years Ago

Teddy carried Monica's limp body to the bedroom and lay her across the bed. He hurriedly ran to the bathroom and told Lil Teddy to finish his bath and get ready for bed.

"Your mom is taking a hot bath. I'll tuck you in tonight."

"Okay, Dad," Lil Teddy innocently replied.

Teddy then locked the bedroom door just in case his son happened to bust in for some odd reason. Looking at his unconscious wife, he was filled with hate and anger. Her continual threats to leave with his son were not taken lightly, and after she angrily spouted those words to him once again, he'd hit his breaking point. He couldn't fathom coming home one day to find out that she had made good on her promise. His son was the only reason he stayed in his unhappy marriage, and he'd be damned if he let Monica dictate whether or not he would be a present or an absentee parent.

The hidden room that he and Monica secretly installed in the new house was the perfect punishment for his wife, he thought. He took the remote out of the dresser drawer, went inside the walk-in closet and opened the hidden entrance behind the enormous shoe display. The compact room was soundproof and resembled a modern jail cell, housing a daybed, a sink, a toilet, and a small television monitor at the top of the wall that could be used to surveil each room in the house. Thanks to Teddy's extensive electrical and plumbing background, he knew the in's and out's of configuring such a space, not knowing at the time that he'd be using it for his own demonic purposes.

Other than Monica and Teddy, no one knew about the closet's transformation and Teddy was going to use that to his advantage. She was still passed out cold when Teddy undressed her down to her underwear and dragged her into their hideaway. He laid her on the daybed, making sure there was nothing inside the room to allow her escape. He threw the thin blanket over her, then locked her inside, not regretting his decision to imprison her.

Putting on his best poker face, he went into his son's room to make sure he was done with his bath. Lil Teddy was just climbing into bed.

"Where's mom? She helps me say my prayers at night."

"Your mom is tired. It's been a long, fun day, and she wanted to take a hot bath and relax. You got something against me helping you with your prayers?" He asked, giving Lil Teddy a playful pouty face.

"No dad," Lil Teddy giggled.

"I wanted to tell you how proud I am of you. Y'all played a good game today. Hard work pays off."

Excitedly, his son exclaimed, "I know! That was soooo fun! You saw how I slid on homeplate? I was running so fast."

"They couldn't catch up to you, son. You did amazing."

"Thanks, Dad." Lil Teddy's heart swelled. He loved his father's praises.

After helping his son with his prayers and making sure he was tucked in, Teddy turned the lights out and shut the door. He made his way back into his bedroom, and as if nothing had transpired, he nonchalantly took a shower and contemplated his next move.

Getting comfortable in the bed for the night, he powered up his tablet and clicked on the link to the monitor inside the hidden room. He saw his outraged wife screaming and banging on the door. Not one sound came through the walls. His lips curled into an evil smirk, then he turned the tablet off, set his alarm for 3:00 a.m., and peacefully went to sleep.

Before the sun graced the sky with its presence, Teddy woke up to his early wake-up call, brushed his teeth, washed his face, and threw on a black hoodie, joggers and running shoes. He tore a piece of fabric from his wife's pink running jacket and put it in his pocket along with her digital stopwatch. After quietly checking on his son, who was still under the Sandman's spell, he crept out the backdoor and through the backyard fence that led to the neighborhood's heavily wooded biking and running trail. He purposely left the cellphones and any trackable devices at home.

He took an early jog through the trail just as Monica would do every other morning at 6:00. Fifteen minutes into his run, he stopped at the top of the trail, went deep into the wooded area off the beaten path, and placed Monica's stopwatch on the ground, roughing it up with his feet so it would look stepped on and gave the appearance of a struggle. Then he placed the fabric from her jacket on a pointy branch from one of the bushes.

Satisfied with what he'd done, he appeared out of the dark brush and lightly jogged back home. It was still early and Lil Teddy hadn't stirred one bit. He looked in on Monica through the monitor and deduced that she'd cried herself to sleep on the daybed that she was sprawled across. When Lil Teddy woke up that beautiful, sunny, Sunday morning, Teddy told him that Monica was out jogging and that they were going fishing for the day. The junior was eager to get going and was none the wiser that his mom was M.I.A. until they got home that evening after a long day on the lake catching fish.

Teddy feigned concern as he called around to family and friends asking if anyone had seen or heard from his wife. Lil Teddy's worry set in, and he had to be consoled. There was never a time where his mom was not present, and he felt sick to his little stomach not knowing where she was. Monica's family showed up to the house questioning Teddy about what could have possibly happened to her, how long had it been since he last saw her, and a slew of other questions. Teddy showed them her phone and advised them that since the trail was literally in their backyard, she never took her phone with her when she went on her morning runs because she didn't want the distraction.

His mom, Felisha, also showed up to the house sincerely concerned about the whereabouts of her daughter-in-law. She was praying that it was all a misunderstanding or miscommunication and that Monica would show up at any moment.

Mark was in an uproar, vowing to cause severe and insufferable pain to anyone who may have harmed his sister. He felt something was off when he didn't hear back from her the previous night when she promised to call him back. She'd been bitching to him about Teddy but told him she'd give him the full story later. Later never came, which he found odd.

Monica's mother, Cynthia, initiated the call to the police. Time was of the essence, and she refused to wait another moment to alert the authorities of her daughter's "disappearance." Her husband, Walt, was already bedridden from a recent heart attack. She didn't know if he would be able to endure any bad news.

When word got out in the neighborhood that Monica hadn't returned home from her morning jog, they all combed the woods looking for her. Of course, Teddy found the first clue—her watch. A detective found the pink fabric. They thought that it was their best clue to try to find Monica. But after a month of no new leads, the urgency to find Monica died down. Her disappearance was just another on a long list of missing persons. The flyers that were posted around the city eventually smeared and dried up from the rain. Some blew away in the wind just like Monica's memory. However, as time went on for some, it stood still for Lil Teddy, Cynthia and Mark who prayed everyday that their beloved would be found safe. Unfortunately, Cynthia's husband's weak heart couldn't take the stress of missing his daughter. After a lengthy night of relentlessly praying for his daughter's return, he closed his eyes and never woke up.

Present Day

With red-rimmed eyes, Monica shot jagged daggers at the man she previously called her husband. Her wide, innocent hazel eyes that were once upon a time full of life were now lifeless. The liveliness had been sucked out of them. Her fine, black hair had grown extremely longer and was pulled back by a lone rubber band. From lack of an appetite, she was rail thin. The glow of her vibrant light brown skin was now dull, and her nails and feet were in desperate need of some TLC.

She asked herself countless times how she missed the signs that he could be so evil and heartless. She knew he was a bit controlling, dismissive and selfish but never to the point that he could treat her like a lab rat and lock her away as a prisoner in their home. She could only imagine the worry that her loved ones were enduring and wondered what excuse Teddy gave them behind her disappearance. Her parents and her brother had to be worried, she thought. Being locked up for so long, her days and nights ran together, and her mental health took a decline. Seclusion in the tight space for an extended period of time had broken her spirit, but the periodic glimpses of Lil Teddy through the monitor that hung overhead in the corner of the soundproof cave kept her hopes high that she'd eventually get out.

Teddy had cameras installed throughout the house and would mentally torture his wife by allowing her to see what he and Lil Teddy were doing. Her heart shattered each time she saw her son. The two things that kept her going were seeing that he was flourishing and that she'd get to put her arms around him again. How and when, she didn't know, but she held on to a tiny nugget of hope.

Other than the short daily previews into their life, Teddy didn't say much to her during his visits to check on her. He'd only supply her with food, water and hygiene essentials and tease her with bits and pieces of Lil Teddy's accomplishments.

"You'd be proud of my son," he'd jokingly tease, "he made an A on his quiz today."

Monica wouldn't respond to his hateful banter. She didn't want to give him the satisfaction of seeing her mentally shrivel. To say she hated Teddy was an understatement. She wanted to set his body on fire and douse him with gasoline over and over until his ashes floated away in the wind. To witness the joy he received from causing her the utmost despair was reprehensible in her eyes.

As he stood over her with the piece of cake, she closed her eyes, tuned him out and silently prayed. She wished that God heard her prayers and would somehow perform a miracle. She didn't know how much more she could mentally endure before she checked out, so she prayed as hard as she could. *There's got to be a way...please please please....she silently begged. This man is vile, evil, heartless...how did I not know this about him?*

He knew he'd gotten inside her head—missing Lil Teddy's birthday again—was the ultimate crush to her soul. He didn't care that she closed her eyes. He laid the napkin with the cake on the edge of the bed, leaving her a memento of the day's event. Figuring, when she decided to open her eyes, she'd be reminded once again. He waltzed out of the tiny room, clicked the lock, and eased back into his bedroom like nothing happened.

Stretching and yawning, he looked in the mirror and said, "Time for bed. It's been a long day."

Kyndall And Teddy

CHAPTER FIVE
KYNDALL AND TEDDY

Sitting outside on the patio of the Italian restaurant enjoying the light evening breeze, Kyndall took a sip of the fine red wine and watched his succulent, manly lips move while he briefly talked about his childhood.

"No, I didn't have a lot of friends growing up," he replied, responding to her question. "When my father died, I was twelve years old, then it was just me and my mom. She picked up what we could, left Ohio and came here to Florida."

"Aw, I'm sorry about your dad. That must have been hard at that age."

"It was, but my mom was strong and our bond became stronger after that."

"If you don't mind me asking, how did he die?" she inquired.

Teddy shook his head, going down memory lane. "A freak accident. He fell down the basement stairs and snapped his neck."

Kyndall put her hands over her mouth. "O no!"

"It's fine. I don't dwell on it," he replied nonchalantly.

What he didn't share was that he was the reason his father was found at the bottom of those steps. Teddy's father was physically abusive to both him and his mother. Teddy came home from school that fateful day and heard his mother crying. From his past experiences, he knew his father was the culprit. The anger welled up inside, and he lured his father to the top of the basement stairs.

"Dad, there's something downstairs. Do you hear that?"

"Boy! Aint nothing down there," his father's irate voice boomed.

"Yes, it is. I hear it."

As soon as his father opened the door leading down to the basement, Teddy mustered up all his adolescent strength and with all his might shoved his father down the stairs. The sounds of his father tumbling down the steps and the final grunt from his fatal fall was still ingrained into his memory. *He ran upstairs to his mom.*

"Dad just fell down the stairs!" His declaration and fake concern rattled his mother.

Felisha, who'd just been on the receiving end of her husband's physical abuse, wiped away the tears, followed her son to the basement and aggressively tried to render aid to her husband. But it was too late. In a panic, she called the EMT. Upon arrival, Tim was pronounced dead. She screamed endlessly, and Teddy cried crocodile tears as they covered his dad's body and wheeled his corpse out of the house. No one was ever the wiser that his son was his "downfall".

"Well, you seem to have overcome…you and your mom. She was very welcoming at the party," Kyndall expressed with a smile.

"That's my mama. She's the best."

"I appreciate you keeping your word and treating me to dinner for helping with the after-party cleanup."

"I'm a man of my word. Plus it gave me an excuse to see you again," he smiled, taking a sip of the wine.

Kyndall blushed. "You didn't need an excuse."

"Okay. I'll take that into consideration for the next date."

"Oh, so there's a next date?" she playfully asked.

"I guess we'll see after the end of the evening."

They raised their glasses to a toast and both took a sip.

Kyndall's phone lit up, and when she noticed that her ex Devon was calling, she ignored the call. The phone lit up once again. Exasperated, she signed, then turned it off.

"Trouble?" Teddy asked.

"Yes and no. My ex can't get over that fact that I was serious about cutting ties this time."

"Oh, I see. But, can I say, I don't blame him?"

"Thanks, but no thanks. He had his time. He didn't use it wisely, so now he has to live with the consequences. Enough about him, though."

"Agreed."

Kyndall and Teddy ate, laughed, talked, and became better acquainted with one another. He learned that she was a junior high school counselor, wanted to have three kids of her own once she met Mr. Right, was best friends with her one and only sibling, Leila, and cherished her nephew, Julian.

She learned that he was the sole owner of Moore Electrical Services, was an all-around handyman, loved fishing, jogging, and spending time with his son and his mom, Felisha.

"So, can I address the pink elephant?" Kyndall boldly asked.

Teddy knew the question was related to Monica's disappearance, so he prepared himself by putting on a poker face and responded.

"Do I need a drink for this?"

"No. No pressure. I was just curious. Have you been dating since IT happened?"

He paused before replying. "Actually, I've been so focused on Lil Teddy and making sure he keeps some form of normalcy that I haven't even had time for anything else. There's a whole lot of gray area...do I remain faithful to a wife who's basically non-existent?" He let that hang for a while as they both contemplated what he'd said.

He then continued. "But meeting you and becoming fast friends, I would hope...it feels good. This is my first outing since IT happened. Thanks for keeping me company this evening."

Smiling, Kyndall responded. "You're welcome. I'm enjoying this time. So, how is Lil Teddy? Did he enjoy his birthday?"

"He had a wonderful time. I appreciate everyone for coming out to celebrate. It meant a lot to him. He's hanging out with my mom right now."

"That's beautiful. He's a sweet boy. How's school going?"

"He's doing pretty good but having some issues with math. His mom was the one who helped him with his homework. That was their thing. Without her around, it's been a bit of a struggle."

"Well, if he needs some help, *and* if you don't mind, I would be happy to tutor him and get him on track. I'm a certified whiz kid when it comes to math. I help some of my students after hours."

"Impressive," Teddy said. "I knew you had brains to match that beauty."

"Flattery...you're too kind. Thank you."

"You're welcome. We may have to take you up on your offer. It's the end of the school year, and he needs to finish strong."

"Let's set something up, and Lil Teddy will be on the right track in no time," she assured.

The two finished their meal, Teddy paid the check, then walked his date to her car. Not wanting to be too forward, he initiated the goodbye hug. They both felt the energy brewing between them while their bodies were gently pressed together. Kyndall appreciated his hard, muscular body, and Teddy admired her softness and the fruity fragrance floating from her hair.

After they slowly ended their embrace, Teddy opened her car door, then stood back while he watched her pull off. A sneaky smile spread across his face, thinking about the things he could do to her. He eventually got in his truck and drove off, not noticing the black BMW parked in the next row.

6

Night Cap

CHAPTER SIX
NIGHT CAP

Making it his personal mission to surveil Teddy, Mark was camped out in the parking lot of the restaurant and watched the exchange between his "brother-in-law" and Kyndall, the beautiful woman who caught his eye at the birthday party. It took everything in him to not get out the car and cause a ruckus. He had no issues with Kyndall, but she would prove to be collateral damage from all the anger he wanted to dump onto Big Ted. He had some nerve gallivanting around town and going out on dates without so much as initiating any type of interest in Monica's whereabouts. Everything surrounding his sister's disappearance never sat right with him and seeing how Teddy was carrying on like a bachelor made his blood boil.

Once he left Lil Teddy's party, Mark made a promise to himself that he was going to be proactive and get some answers to hopefully find out what happened to his sister. If following Teddy around was what he had to do, then so be it. He followed Teddy from a distance, and from the route he took, figured he was on his way back home. He was going to end his tail but hung back a little longer at the curb of the cul-de-sac, watching Teddy pull up into the driveway.

A car was sitting in front of Teddy's house, and once Teddy turned off his truck, a woman hurriedly got out of her car and approached him. Squinting his eyes to get a better look at the female, Mark realized that it was the team mom, Yasmine, whom his sister mentioned was possibly sleeping with Teddy. He'd seen her on a few occasions when he would catch his nephew's game. He also recalled seeing her at the birthday party. Mark couldn't believe the audacity of both Teddy and Yasmine.

He watched the interaction as Yasmine apparently talked rapidly with her hands like she was angry while Teddy nonchalantly regarded her until he rushed her to the doorstep, unlocked the door, then invited her inside. Mark became even more incensed. Teddy's outright disrespect was over the roof and he'd had enough. He knew he couldn't blow a gasket just yet. Lil Teddy had permission to spend the day with him and his mother soon, so he'd keep his cool for just a while longer. Keeping his promise to Lil Teddy trumped whatever feelings he had for Teddy. However, he was no longer going to sweep Monica's disappearance under the rug. Finding her was top priority. He owed it to his sister, her son, and his parents.

***

Reluctantly allowing Yasmine to enter his home, Teddy didn't want his neighbors to see her in front of his yard causing a scene. He was frustrated with her insistence and her nerve to pop up at his house unannounced. He walked to the kitchen with Yasmine following behind, threw his car keys down on the island, turned around with folded arms and scolded her with his look.

"Yasmine, what the hell is this all about? You're really testing my patience lately and acting out of character. Since when do you start coming to my home uninvited? This is not what we do," he chastised.

She met his gaze. "Four years," she held up four manicured fingers. "Four...we've been enjoying each other. I've been patient, waiting in the wings for you to finally leave your wife. And now since she's gone, I'm still waiting in the wings. You haven't answered any of my calls or texts all day. Have I just been wasting my time, Teddy...huh?"

With pouty lips and eyes begging for attention, she slithered toward him. She helped uncross his arms and softened his resolve by putting her arms around his neck.

He looked down into her intense green eyes. "So, you feel like you've been wasting your time?"

"I'm just saying. Don't you think it's time?"

"Considering what my family has been going through for the past couple of years, I would think you would understand."

"I did, until I saw that your attention has shifted. You've been acting different since I saw you talking to that girl at the birthday party."

"Are you keeping tabs on me? And where's Antonio while you're over here checking for me?"

"My son is fine…he's with my mom," she replied dismissively. "I'm not keeping tabs on you, but I refuse to be put on the backburner while you pursue new interests."

"Stop being paranoid. You have nothing to worry about. I was just being hospitable to all my guests. If you took that as something more, then that's on you," he lied.

"O really? Well, since you're such a hospitable type of guy, can you show me some hospitality?" She turned on her enticing switch. "I've been having this ache that I need you to massage."

On her tippy toes, she tickled his earlobe with the tip of her tongue, knowing it was one of his many weak spots. Furthering her advances, she glided her hand down his chest and his hard abs, then stopped at his waistband. His heart raced a bit. Saying "no" to Yasmine was never something he was able to accomplish. She took advantage of the moment and seductively stepped away from him while keeping her eyes trained on his.

She undid each strap from the sundress and let it fall to the floor, revealing her tight, svelte body. She saw him take a deep breath as his eyes traveled up her long, tan legs to her red, lace panties and her all-natural C cups that were screaming for his attention.

Noticing that his body was responding to her liking, she turned around, removed her panties while slowly bending over to give him a bird's eye view of all she had to offer. Leaving her panties on the kitchen floor, she slowly sauntered to his bedroom, knowing that he was right on her heels and taking in the tempting view.

Teddy always found Yasmine irresistible, and that moment was no different from any other time, but he'd just returned home from seeing Kyndall, and she was still fresh on his mind. But if Yasmine was screaming for hospitality, then that's exactly what he was going to give her.

Recalling that he'd left his secret remote and his tablet on his bed to keep his eyes on Monica, he quickly rushed to his bedroom door to make sure Yasmine didn't accidentally hit any buttons. He picked her up, and she straddled him while planting kisses on his neck. After he laid her down in the middle of the bed, he inconspicuously shoved the remote and the tablet underneath his pillow while she expertly unbuckled his pants.

After helping him unleash the very thing that she desired, Yasmine was beyond delighted when he pleasingly punished her to no end. She welcomed each deep stroke as if it were the first, looking at him with lust and love in her eyes. She misinterpreted his looks to match what she was feeling; yet when Teddy looked down at her, he envisioned Kyndall's pretty face, soft skin and sensuous brown eyes staring back at him. His thoughts of Kyndall spurred him into an intensity he hadn't felt in a long time.

The sweet and explosive session literally came to an end, and Yasmine had a gigantic smile spread across her face. She wanted Teddy to bask in the afterglow with her and wrap his arms around her while spooning, but he had other plans. He quickly gathered her garments, cleaned up, and made her do the same before walking her to the door.

"My mom will be bringing Lil Teddy home soon," he partly explained his haste in seeing her out.

"I get it, Teddy," she said, looking into his eyes. "I hope tonight reminds you of what's waiting for you." She kissed him on the lips, exited the house, and happily sashayed to her car.

***

Still camped out on the corner in his car, Mark clocked the time of Yasmine's departure. He was no dummy and knew exactly what those two had been up to. Thirty minutes was more than enough time to get the sheets dirty. He was furious but adamant to keep his cool for the time being. *Teddy is going to get what he has coming to him if it's the last thing I do*, Mark vowed.

***

The angry, hot tears rolled down Monica's face. She was beyond disgusted and outraged. The hatred ran deep for Teddy, and after what she'd just witnessed, Yasmine was added to that list. Monica never had concrete proof that her husband was messing around with the team tramp, but she instinctively knew. She'd confronted Teddy about it on numerous occasions, but he would deny, ignore, or become belligerent.

"How could he! The bed we shared. My home. My son. My life! Whyyyyyyyyyy! Teddy...whyyyyyyyyy!" She screamed and banged on the door of the insulated cell until her voice became hoarse and her tired malnourished body gave out.

7

Beast Mode

C HAPTER SEVEN
BEAST MODE

"Hey sis."

Kyndall strolled into the gym dressed professionally in her work attire—a coral-colored blouse, black slacks and matching pumps with her hair up in a bun. She tried to get Leila's attention, but her sister was busy mixing a smoothie in a loud blender and side eyeing the two women in the gym who were obviously flirting with Eric and his trainee, Ian.

Beast Mode, the gym jointly owned by Eric and Leila, was booming with after-work clients. Leila, who had her hair up in a messy ponytail and wearing a black *Beast Mode* t-shirt with black biker shorts, worked the smoothie bar whipping up healthy, frothy concoctions, poured the elixir into a cup and handed it to the sweating man.

"Thanks, Carlos. See you tomorrow."

Carlos smiled and lifted his cup in response. "See you later."

Clearing her throat, "Oh...once again...hey sis." Kyndall reiterated.

"Hey K. I'm sorry. I meant to speak back, but I was preoccupied," she said while continuing to eye the two thirsties who were hounding her husband.

Kyndall looked over at the two women dressed in matching tight yoga shorts and sports bras standing by while Eric spotted Ian who was sweating profusely from lifting a significant amount of weight while doing bench presses.

Chuckling, she said, "Girl, I know you're not letting those two get you in your feelings. Eric is ignoring them anyway.

Leila swatted the air in response, grabbed the blender pitcher, and proceeded to wash it in the sink.

"Normally, I'm okay, but lately I've been getting this funny feeling. I trust my husband, but he's still a man. A man can only take so much temptation from these beautiful women constantly throwing themselves at him."

Kyndall sat her purse down on the counter. "Are you serious, Leila? That man over there cherishes you. He worships the ground your crusty feet walk on."

Laughing out loud, Leila nodded. "I don't know why I'm tripping. But for real, those two are about to get on my last nerve. This is their second time here, and they've been eye humping my man relentlessly."

Pointing in his direction, "Look at your husband," Kyndall instructed. "He's not even paying them heifers no mind."

Leila knew Eric was one-hundred percent professional, so she decided to ignore the duo and focus on her sister.

"You're right," she agreed, then changed the subject. "So, what's going on with you, sis? You look nice."

"Thanks. Not too much, but then again..." Kyndall grinned. "Guess who treated me to dinner yesterday?"

Leila shook her head, already knowing the answer to that question. "Sis, do you think that's wise? You know what Teddy and his son have been going through. That's a slippery slope you may not want to climb."

"It's all innocent...just having a little fun, besides, have you seen him? That man is fine fine," she said, fanning herself.

"Sorry, I didn't notice. I was too busy concentrating on my own fine specimen of a man." Leila looked over at Eric who continued to be oblivious to his adoring fans.

"Please! You're married, not blind. And stop hating...I'm trying to get like you someday."

"If you ask me, then I would suggest you look elsewhere. Technically, that man is still married and has unresolved issues. I'm sure you have multiple options."

As soon as Leila said that, Kyndall's phone rang loudly in her purse. She quickly retrieved it, and saw her ex-boyfriend, Devon calling. She showed Leila the screen of the incoming call.

"Speaking of options," she said, rolling her eyes and hitting "decline" on the call.

"Is he still bothering you," Leila asked with concern.

"Girl, yes. I was having dinner with Teddy, and he was texting and calling non stop like he knew what I was doing."

"I don't like that, K. He had a good thing and ruined it. I guess he thought you were gonna sit around and continue to deal with his infidelity."

"Exactly! I deserve way better than that."

"Yes, you do. But Teddy is not it. Don't get me wrong, I like Teddy, and his son is a sweetheart, but you need somebody that doesn't have all that baggage."

Kyndall knew her sister had her best interest at heart, but it went in one ear and out the other. She was enjoying being newly single and wanted to have fun dating until Mr. Right showed up at her door. Her phone blared again. She huffed and rolled her eyes.

"OMG! Will he stop already?"

Leila grew even more concerned. "Maybe you need to address that and make it clear to him that you're done."

"I did. I might have to change my number." She shook her head.

"I don't know if I like that stalkerish vibe he's giving off."

"Devon is the least of my concerns. He better go cuddle up with the last trick he was talking to."

Leila shook her head then noticed one of the women walk up to Eric to ask for assistance with the adductor machine.

"Oh no....she's clearly trying to shoot her shot. I'm bout to go over there."

Leila was getting ready to walk around the counter and head in Eric's direction when Kyndall blocked her.

"No, Sis. Look."

They both watched as Eric got his colleague, Casey, and introduced her to the females for assistance, then he casually walked off to continue his workout session with Ian. Casey took over and instructed the women on proper use of the gym equipment. Clearly, the ladies were not interested as they both had a deflated look on their faces. Kyndall and Leila laughed while watching the events from afar.

"See what I told you. Eric knew exactly how to handle that."

Leila beamed proudly. "That's my boo." She traveled back around the counter. "Want a smoothie?"

"Sure," Kyndall answered, looking down at her ringing phone. Her face lit up. It was Teddy. "But give me a second." She walked off while Leila threw the ingredients in the blender to make her sister's favorite apple-berry smoothie.

"Hi," Kyndall cheerily sang into the phone as she stepped outside the building to take the call.

"Good evening. You sound in good spirits. I take it you had a good day."

"Oh, you know…the usual…dealing with adolescents and their perpetual end-of-the-world problems, but other than that, it's been a good day. What about you?"

"Hmmm…let's see. Other than working on rewiring a client's garage and wondering if you would take me up on my offer to join me for some bowling on Saturday, it's been a good day as well."

"Smooth. I see how you slid that in."

That's not the only thing I want to slide in, Teddy thought to himself.

"Let me check my calendar." Kyndall paused for effect. "Just kidding. Nobody's knocking down my door to hangout, so you're in luck."

"I like the sound of that—not that no one's knocking down your door, but that you can hang out. Either way, it works out in my favor," he laughed. "Should I pick you up?"

"Sure. I'll be at my sister's, so you can just pick me up from there."

"Sounds like a plan. See you soon, beautiful."

Grinning from ear to ear, she disconnected the call. Leila noticed the spotlight that was shining on her sister when she stepped back inside.

"Uhm, who has you all in a daze?"

"I'm not in a daze," Kyndall tried to downplay her elation. "That was Teddy. He wants to hangout on Saturday."

Leila handed her sister the smoothie and gave her a reprimanding look. "Just be careful, sis. Just be careful."

8

Revelation

C HAPTER EIGHT
REVELATION

Reluctantly, Teddy drove his son to Cynthia's house to spend the day with his grandmother and Uncle Mark. For the past two years, he only allowed Lil Teddy to see his grandmother and uncle while he supervised and at games and public events. He couldn't risk them trying to brainwash his son or pry information out of him. He figured enough time had passed that he could be comfortable knowing that there was nothing Lil Teddy could say or do to jeopardize the secret. He also didn't want to go back on his promise to his son by not allowing him to spend time with Monica's family.

It was no mystery that he and Mark were not friends. Teddy could only imagine all the things that Monica told her brother over the years to make him out to be the bad guy, like he wasn't good enough for her. He knew that Mark was instrumental in trying to get his sister to leave and take Lil Teddy with her. *Not on your life*, Teddy thought. *They thought they could run off with my son and I would be okay with that. I had to let them know who's in charge.*

Cynthia must have been looking out the window because she popped out the door as soon as they pulled up in front of her house. Teddy looked over at his son and saw the joy in his face and his eagerness to hop out of the truck. As much as it pained him to admit it, his son adored his maternal grandmother and uncle. However, Teddy had to draw a line in the sand just to assert his authority over the situation.

Lil Teddy was elated to see his grandmother. Her face, her stature, everything about her reminded him of his mother, and it subconsciously gave him an inner peace and happiness. He ran into her welcoming embrace that always made him feel warm and fuzzy on the inside. He loved his dad and his grandma Felisha, but the unconditional, pure love he received from his grandma Cynthia and Uncle Mark was indescribable. He missed the days that all five of them were at the house together—Monica, Cynthia, Mark and his grandpa, Walt. The family was close, loving, and they had fun together playing games, making jokes, and just enjoying each other's company.

In his eyes, Grandpa Walt was the best. He had a bubbly and comedic personality. When Lil Teddy was four and five years old, his grandfather would pull magical quarters out of his grandson's ears, or so Lil Teddy thought. His young mind was blown at the magic trick. "Wow!" Lil Teddy exclaimed each time. When Grandpa Walt died, Lil Teddy took it hard, but his grandma Cynthia reassured him that his grandfather would always be around watching over him. She gave him his grandfather's coveted coin collection, and he felt close to his grandfather everytime he looked at it.

Cynthia held onto her grandson for a minute as a wave of emotion washed over her and a tear rolled down her cheek. Seeing the growing, young man that he was becoming, she knew her husband and daughter would be proud.

Teddy walked to the foot of the steps and dropped Lil Teddy's backpack down.

"Cynthia," he nodded.

"Hi, Teddy. Thank you." The emotions in her eyes spoke volumes.

"You're welcome. I'll pick him up around eleven, if that's okay."

"It's totally fine if he spends the night."

"We have plans tomorrow. I'll pick him up," Teddy unemotionally stated. "Have fun, son," he said before walking back to his truck.

Cynthia dismissed Teddy's borderline rude behavior. "Guess what I made?" she asked her grandson as they stepped into the house.

Lil Teddy inhaled deeply, taking in the scrumptious scent of his favorite dessert. "Chocolate chip cookies! Can I have some?" He could hardly wait. His grandmother made the best homemade chocolate chip cookies. He put his bag down in the living room and hightailed it to the kitchen.

"How can I tell my boy no," she said, planting a kiss on his forehead. While putting a couple of warm cookies on a napkin, she informed him that Mark was out back grilling hot dogs and hamburgers. His face lit up even more.

With one cookie in hand and the other stuffed in his mouth, he ran to the patio door, burst outside and greeted his uncle, who looked relaxed in a black crew neck tee, basketball shorts and Nike slides.

"Hey, nephew!" Mark was happy to see his one and only nephew. He put down the tongs that he was using to flip the hotdogs, and they engaged in their signature handshake.

"After we eat, are you ready for me to spank that butt on that new game?"

Lil Teddy found his uncle's statement hilarious. "Uncle Mark, you can't beat me. I'm nice with the controllers."

"Nice?" Mark laughed. "Who are you? You sound like a grown man. I see I'm gonna have to show you who's the man around here."

"Okay, but don't say I didn't warn you." He stuffed the other cookie in his mouth.

The only thing Mark could do after that was shake his head and laugh at his nephew's confidence and unwavering disposition.

The three of them sat down at the table to eat and catch up. Lil Teddy gave them an update on how his classes were going and about a cute girl at his school who he was smitten with. Cynthia got a little emotional and momentarily excused herself from the table, gathered herself, then came back. Seeing how fast her grandson was growing up and not having her daughter or her husband around was a little too much to bear. Lil Teddy may have looked like his father, but his smile, his demeanor and his talkative nature was all Monica's genes.

She reached across the table and laid her hand on top of his. "You know if there's anything you ever need or if you just want to talk or see our faces, you know we're here for you, okay?"

"Yes, ma'am."

"Just because we don't spend as much time together like we used to doesn't mean we don't love you, okay."

The glassy look in Lil Teddy's eyes conveyed that her sentiments were touching him, but he was trying to be tough.

"Okay, Grandma."

Before the moment got too awkward or emotional, Mark interjected.

"So, did all your buddies have a good time at your party?"

"Yes! That was the best!"

Lil Teddy began to mindlessly ramble on about how much fun he had, the gifts he received, and his dad's new friend, Miss Kyndall, who helped clean up and gave him some money as a gift at the end of the day. Mark's ears perked up at the mention of her name. It was too much going on at the time of the party, and he couldn't recall her name. He made a mental note to look her up.

"That was nice of her," Cynthia added, noticing Mark's slight attitude shift.

Teddy's extracurricular activities were always a sore spot for Mark. Monica used to vent about her husband's treatment, and Mark would urge her to leave. Cynthia, however, would encourage her to stick it out, try counseling or whatever it took to keep her marriage. Thinking back on those conversations, Cynthia believed that she should have listened more to what her daughter needed and wanted. Coming from an era where women stood by their husbands regardless of their indiscretions, Cynthia was not equipped to give her daughter any advice to the contrary.

After witnessing firsthand how Teddy used Monica's disappearance to drive a wedge in between her relationship with her only grandson, she regretted not agreeing with Monica's wishes to leave him. He was clearly a control freak, so she could only imagine the full spectrum of what her daughter had to endure. But if she had to play nice with Teddy to continue to see her grandchild, then that's what she would do. She just had to make sure that Mark kept his cool, but that was easier said than done.

Mark got up from the table and returned. He put a phone down on the table.

"Nephew, this is for you. This is your other gift, but it's our secret. I want you to make sure you have my number and your grandma's number on speed dial. If you ever need to reach us, you call us. You hear me?"

Lil Teddy nodded. "Yes, sir."

"I want you to keep it in a safe place. I know it's not good to keep secrets from your parents, but under the circumstances, I want to make sure you'll always be able to reach us. I want to make sure you're safe. Can you do that for me?"

"I understand, Uncle Mark. It's our secret."

"Turn it on, so I can make sure you know how to use it."

Mark instructed his nephew on how to use the phone and made him send him a test text message. Mark's phone lit up with a picture of him and Monica as his screensaver. Lil Teddy looked down at his uncle's phone, noticing the picture of Uncle Mark and Monica. Before Mark could dim the screensaver, Lil Teddy picked up the phone. He stared at it for a few seconds before the picture faded.

"That's you and my mom."

"Yes, it is," Mark solemnly replied.

Lil Teddy's next statement threw them both for a loop.

"That's the pink jacket my dad threw away," he matter-of-factly stated.

Cynthia gasped and put her hand over her shocked mouth.

Mark knew how much his sister loved that pink jacket. She'd wear it during her jogs and was supposedly wearing it the day she went missing, they theorized from the material that was found in the trail. Mark had initially found it odd that she was jogging that morning because they had a conversation the day before to meet up for breakfast to discuss her exit plan from her marriage. After the material from her jacket was found in the trail, Mark assumed that maybe his sister changed her mind and decided to go for a run after all. He was still trying to piece together all the information since that day. His mistrust of Teddy had him thinking that it was all to convenient.

Not wanting to alarm Lil Teddy or make it seem like what he said was urgent, Mark calmly asked, "Monica loved that jacket. When did your dad throw it away?"

"When we went fishing. He put it in the dumpster with his work boots. He said they were old and he had to clean out his truck so we could make room for all the fish we were going to catch."

"Did you catch a lot of fish?"

"No, we only caught a few small ones. I was going to show Mom what we caught, but when we got home...," he bent his head down, not wanting to remember that horrible day.

"It's okay, I know." Mark patted Lil Teddy on his back.

Cynthia was still shocked and thinking all kinds of things. Her hands were shaking, so she got up from the table and went into the bathroom while Mark pretended that everything was cool and continued to engage Lil Teddy, despite the rage boiling up inside of him.

Changing the subject, Mark asked, "You finished eating? Cause I'm about to whoop you on this game."

"I hate to see my uncle cry, but that's what's about to happen," Lil Teddy's sadness quickly changed to jovial as he got into gamer mode.

"Oh, you're funny lil man."

Mark tried to keep his attitude in check. What Lil Teddy had just revealed had his mind spiraling out of control, and he couldn't wait to see Teddy face to face. Something had to be done, and he was not going to wait around any longer until he got the answers he needed as to what happened to his sister. He just had to get through the evening with his nephew; however, the ticking time bomb going off inside his head was going to make that very difficult for him.

***

Teddy couldn't help but admire Kyndall from the back as she bent over and tossed the glossy, metallic-colored bowling ball down the smooth lane. The tight, stretchy blue jeans she wore that looked like they were painted on her body had him in a trance. His daze continued when she turned around after getting a strike and bounced up and down in victory causing her perfect C cups that were trapped inside her tank top to join in the celebration. The smile on her face and the liveliness in her eyes enhanced the complete package.

"Yes!" Kyndall expressed with her hands in the air to signify her win.

"I only let you win because you're a girl," he joked.

"Oh really. Is that the new loser speech?"

"Wow...that stings," he responded, feigning hurt feelings.

"I'm sorry. I promise I won't be so rough the next time."

There was a glimmer in his eyes. "I like it rough."

"Oh, do tell. By the way, we are still talking about bowling, right?"

He smiled and nodded repeatedly. "Yea, bowling, yea."

Kyndall was amused. "You're too funny. This has been fun, though. I really needed this down time. I appreciate this...what is this...a date?"

Teddy got closer to her and looked down into her pretty, light-brown eyes. "Yes, it is, and I wouldn't mind taking you on another."

The sparks flew, and Kyndall was smitten.

"And I wouldn't mind accepting your offer."

"That's music to my ears. On another note, can I take you up on your offer to tutor my son in math?"

"You most certainly can. I'll look at my schedule and let you know what days are good for me, and we can coordinate something."

"Sounds good," Teddy replied, looking down at the empty glasses and the basket of fries and wings. "Did you want another drink before we get our shoes and head out?"

"One more for the road, and then duty calls. I know you have to pick up your son."

"The life of a single dad."

As soon as he said those words, the pink elephant re-appeared. Was he truly single? How long was long enough before he gave up on the possibility of his wife returning? Did he miss her? Was their harmless dating going to turn into something serious? There were a lot of unanswered questions floating around in Kyndall's head, but she quickly shrugged them off, choosing not to ruin the evening and dwell on it. She'd revisit those questions another time. In the meantime, she was going to enjoy the moment and not overthink it.

9

Confrontation

C HAPTER NINE
CONFRONTATION

After letting Lil Teddy beat him in a few rounds of the fighting game they were playing, Mark had to set out and find out which bowling alley Teddy had gone to. He couldn't concentrate on anything other than what his nephew unknowingly revealed. He played it off like nothing was wrong and even found out from Cynthia that Teddy said he was going bowling. Mark left Lil Teddy to spend the remaining hours with his grandmother, who fixed them some popcorn and found a good movie for them to watch. Cynthia was still shaken, but they both kept their composure for the sake of Lil Teddy. She would normally stop Mark from doing something impulsive, but considering what they had just learned, she could no longer keep him on a leash.

Once Mark reiterated to Lil Teddy the importance of keeping his phone hidden and that they would be in constant contact, he was on a mission to find Teddy. There were a couple of popular bowling alleys in the nearby area, and after unsuccessfully trying the first one, he went to the other one. When he spotted Teddy's matte black truck in the parking lot, his heartbeat quickened. He wanted to go guns blazing inside and demand answers. His rational mind told him to wait until Teddy exited the building, but his irrational mind said, "to hell with that."

He wanted answers, and he wanted them immediately. Mark got out of his car and stomped his way towards the entrance. Coincidentally, as soon as he got to the door, Teddy and Kyndall were approaching the exit. Teddy pushed out the door only to see Mark's angry face.

What the hell is he doing here? Was the first question that popped in Teddy's head.

Kyndall looked at the two men staring at each other like two boxers in the ring ready to square up. *O no...this can't be good,* she nervously thought.

The smug look on Teddy's face sent Mark into a tailspin. All the pent up anger he'd been holding onto for the past couple of years had broken the seal. He felt that not only was Teddy hiding something, but he was also obviously openly dating Kyndall and sneaking around with Yasmine. Mark could no longer contain himself.

"What did you do to my sister?! You asshole!" he screamed at the top of his lungs and followed it up by hitting Teddy with his hammer fist, sending his crashing backwards into the glass door and shattering it into pieces.

"Teddy!" Kyndall shrieked. Her first inclination was to help him up, but she was frozen in place by Mark's aggressiveness and didn't want to get hurt.

"Get up! Get some more of this!" Mark yelled, watching Teddy groan as he tried to get up from the floor.

People were standing around with their camera phones obviously recording, and Kyndall wanted to find a rock and hide underneath. Instead, she helped a delirious Teddy to his feet. He was adamant about not being outdone, so he swung at Mark with as much strength as he could muster after being struck. Mark, being a few inches shorter, ducked and came back with a body shot to Teddy's side. The pain shot through his body.

"Stop!" Kyndall screamed.

She tried to grab Teddy's arm and pull him away, but her attempts were fruitless. He pulled away from her grasp and latched onto Mark, pulling him into a headlock.

"Teddy...stop! The police are coming!" Kyndall tried to de-escalate the situation before the police arrived.

The sirens were blaring in the distance.

Mark wiggled out of Teddy's hold, and they fought head to head—blow for blow. Teddy was taller and bigger, but Mark's angry strength was hard to combat. Each punch rocked Teddy to his core; however, he refused to let Mark get the best of him in front of his date. Mark was like a feisty chihuahua...relentless and vicious.

By the time the police arrived and jumped out of their cars, Kyndall was relieved and distraught. One officer grabbed Teddy and the other manhandled Mark and quickly cuffed him.

"It was his fault!" Kyndall yelled at the officer while pointing at Mark.

"Yea, I got it on camera," a spectator added.

"That man was minding his business when all of a sudden..." another witness interjected.

"Everybody get back!" the officer demanded.

They each led Teddy and Mark to the squad cars. Angry and embarrassed, Teddy couldn't believe he was caught on camera fighting outside the bowling alley and being led away in handcuffs. The back of his head was tender from his backwards fall into the glass door. He couldn't tell if he was bleeding or not. His face felt like he'd been hit with a couple of pool balls, and his shirt was torn and hanging off like he'd wrestled with a bear and lost. He sorely underestimated Mark's strength.

"This aint over with!" Mark threatened.

"Sir, I'd advise you to remain silent. Making threats will only cause more problems for you," the officer said before stuffing Mark in the backseat of the cruiser.

Mark was so drunk with anger that he could care less what was going on around him. His laser focus was on Teddy and Teddy only.

After confining Mark, the officer took Kyndall to the side to get the who, what, when, why and how. She explained what happened while the officer took notes. Teddy watched her plead his case, and her concern was endearing; however, he was still reeling from the embarrassment of his current situation.

Once they concluded that Mark was the instigator and the aggressor, they let Teddy go. He and Kyndall finally got into the truck to leave, while the bowling alley staff was left behind to pick up the pieces and patch up the doorway. While in the truck, the quiet of the night had returned, but the damage that had been done was loud. Teddy was deep in thought. *Why was Mark so enraged? What did he and Lil Teddy talk about?* Question after question popped up in his head. Something had to have been said for Mark to take it to that extreme. He could only guess at that moment.

The ride was eerily quiet, and Kyndall didn't know what to say. She could tell that the wheels in Teddy's mind were rolling, and she wanted to give him his mental space, however, she decided to break the ice.

"I'm sorry that happened to you."

He looked over and saw the sincerity in her eyes. "Thanks. No need for you to apologize for his immature behavior. Maybe some time behind bars will make him think twice about flying off the handle like an immature adolescent. I'm most definitely pressing charges. That was totally uncalled for. If anyone needs to apologize, it's me. I wanted to take you out for an enjoyable evening, then that happened."

"If it's any consolation, I did have fun. It's not your fault what happened. I will let you make it up to me, though. Buuut, you gotta let me pick the place," she giggled.

"Say less."

Teddy had initially planned on picking his son up once he dropped Kyndall off to her car, but he had to get Lil Teddy away from his in-laws. From Mark's actions, Teddy deduced that they were pumping his son for information. *What on earth could Lil Teddy have said?*

Once he got to Cynthia's house, he jumped out of the truck and banged on the door.

"Oh, I thought I had a little more time to spend with my grandson," Cynthia said after answering the door.

"You need to ask your son why I'm here early. Nevermind...you can't. He's in the county jail," Teddy sharply replied.

"Dear Lord!" Cynthia took in Teddy's disheveled appearance, and it wasn't hard to guess what happened.

Asking questions or trying to reason with him was useless, so she calmly gathered Lil Teddy and his belongings and ushered him to the door. Whatever Mark had done, she knew Teddy was going to use to his advantage. She kissed her grandson and told him how much she loved him.

"Love you too, Gran. See you again, soon."

"Hmmph," Teddy mumbled.

"Hey Lil Teddy," Kyndall greeted him when he got inside the car.

"Hi, Miss Kyndall. I had fun. Me and Gran just watched a movie and had some popcorn. She made my favorite cookies and I even beat my Uncle Mark in three games," he excitedly expressed, unaware of any prior tension.

Kyndall cringed when Mark's name was mentioned. Teddy remained silent.

"That's wonderful that you enjoyed yourself," she responded.

"Yes, I can't wait for the next time!"

She looked over at Teddy and could tell from his facial expression that "next time" may not happen anytime soon. The rest of the ride was silent. Lil Teddy was engrossed in his handheld game, and Kyndall decided to just let sleeping dogs lie for the moment. Teddy dropped her off in front of her sister's house where her car was parked and walked her to her car door.

"I'm sorry how our date ended, but like I said earlier, I'm going to make it up to you."

Kyndall cocked her head to the side and looked at him with understanding. "I know. Just go home, get your son situated, then take a relaxing soak in the tub."

"I just might do that. I have a splitting headache."

"Are you sure you don't need to go to the hospital?"

"Positive. I'll call you tomorrow about your schedule."

She nodded in agreement. He wanted to kiss her luscious lips, but the timing was off, and he didn't want his son to witness. Instead, he opened the door for her, letting her ease inside. He stood watch until she cranked up the engine and drove off.

Soon after, Teddy and his junior arrived home, each in their own thoughts. Teddy needed a moment to gather himself before questioning his son about his visit with Cynthia and Mark.

"Go get cleaned up and ready for bed, son. We'll talk about how your visit went in the morning."

"Okay, Dad." Eager to get to his room, Lil Teddy did as he was told.

Once inside the confines of his space, he dug the phone from his bag and examined it. The picture of his mom and Uncle Mark was saved on the screensaver. He looked at it for a long while. The smile on his mom's face caused him to miss her even more. Being at his Gran's house gave him the opportunity to feel closer to his mom, but now that he was back home in his private space, he felt disconnected again. His eyes turned misty and a tear slid down his face. He sent a text to his grandmother and uncle.

I love you. I had fun and can't wait to come over again

As his uncle instructed, he shut the phone off, placed it back in the bottom of his bag, and put the bag in his closet. He then got down on his knees like his mother taught him and prayed to God that she would come back home.

In the master suite, Teddy was seething and beyond furious. Getting beat up in front of Kyndall while bystanders recorded was all out humiliating. He wanted to punch a wall or three. After heatedly pacing across the floor a few times, he grabbed his remote, went into the closet and paid his wife a visit. She was lying on the bed, staring blankly at the ceiling. Teddy rushed towards her and unleashed his misplaced anger at her.

"You see this?!"

Monica didn't respond or even look his way.

"Your fuckin' brother!"

At the mention of her brother, she snapped her head in his direction and saw the fire in his eyes along with the bruises on his face.

"He thinks he can put his hands on me, and I'll just fold?!" He bent down and got close up in her face where she could smell the vodka he had obviously drank. The fresh batch of hate in his eyes were new.

What had Mark done? she wondered.

"Well, I got something for his ass!"

Teddy wrapped his fingers around Monica's neck. She just knew that he finally grew the balls to end her life and take her out of her misery. However, he had something far more sinister in store for her. With one hand firmly gripped around her neck, he used the other hand to unbuckle his pants. Finding herself unable to speak, her tears spoke for her. Teddy was unfazed. His anger towards Mark was misguided and landed on Monica.

He ripped the cloth barrier from her lean body and angrily plunged beyond the depths of her comfort, killing her soul with each silent and powerful thrust. She wanted to die. She wanted to scream out for him to kill her quickly. She no longer had a voice. With her power depleted and feeling like a rag doll, she silently cried and endured brutal, carnal penetration until he transferred his anger from one being to another. His heavy breathing and the clink of his belt buckle filled the tiny space. Once he finished, he got up, filled the small sink with water, wet the washcloth, wiped himself, then threw the cloth at his wife, He exited the enclosure, leaving her to cry herself into a deeper depression.

***

On the ride home, Kyndall had time to reflect on the night's events and couldn't believe all that had transpired. She felt bad for Teddy. They were really hitting it off until Mark showed up and ruined the night. Maybe her sister was right, and she didn't need to insert herself into their family dynamics. There was obviously a lot going on that she was not privy to, but on the other hand, she found herself somewhat intrigued by Teddy and wanted to explore their new friendship further.

She pulled into the driveway of her townhouse and saw that she had uninvited company. *I know the hell he did not!* She shook her head. She had enough drama for the night and was not in the mood for more. Taking her time getting out of the car to contemplate how she planned on handling him, she finally stepped out. Devon leaned against the side of the car watching her watch him. The tight jeans on her body had him missing what was underneath.

"Looking good in them jeans," he expressed.

To Kyndall, Devon was tall, dark, and handsome personified and was looking extra handsome and casual in a short-sleeve collared shirt, a pair of jeans that hung loosely on his tall frame and a fresh pair of Nike's; however, she was not impressed. She annoyingly rolled her eyes and questioned why he was there.

"Devon, it's late and I'm tired. What do you want? And why are you hanging outside my place like a stalker?"

"Baby—"

"Don't baby me. You gave up the right to call me that when you couldn't decide where you wanted to lay your pipe."

"Bae...Kyndall, I told you I was confused. I didn't know what I wanted. I know what I want now. I miss you, baby. I need you in my life. I've been miserable."

"It's a little too late for that now. You don't get to decide how long I have to tolerate your indecisiveness and indiscretions. I gave you my all. What did I get in return? Drama! Trust me...I'm good now."

"So, I can't come in and plead my case? I don't plan on giving up, Kyndall."

"Sorry, but you no longer have the power to decide that. It's over, Devon."

"Just like that? Where have you been? You got another man in your ear? I'm telling you now, Kyndall, if I see another man in your face, it might not go over so well."

"You've got a whole lotta nerves. Who I see and plan to spend my time with is MY business! This conversation is over. I suggest you leave now before I call the police."

With his arms splayed out, Devon questioned her intent. "Oh, it's like that?"

Taking a firm stance, she affirmed. "Yes! You made it like that. Now, if you'll excuse me...I'm gone."

She turned to walk away, but Devon grabbed her arm and continued to plead.

"I'm telling you now, I'm not giving up. And whoever you're out here gallivanting through the city with, better watch his back."

"Get your hands off me!" She snatched her arm away and marched to her front door, opening it, then slamming it shut.

She was slightly rattled but had refused to allow Devon to see her sweat. He had taken more than enough of her time and energy over the years, and she was completely done. His attempts at a reconciliation were falling on deaf ears. She stepped out of her shoes and looked out the window to make sure he was gone. She saw the taillights of his Maserati as he drove away, but she had the unsettling feeling that he would not give up so easily. Her phone buzzed with a message from Devon.

I still love you

Kyndall threw the phone on the bed and sighed. "It's been a loooong day," she expressed to herself before taking a shower and calling it a night.

Suspicions

CHAPTER TEN
SUSPICIONS

Leila stared at the lipstick stain on her husband's shirt.

"This isn't my color," she spoke out loud.

She tried to remember the day he wore that particular shirt. To her recollection, it was the day he said he was meeting his brother for dinner, and that they had to catch up.

"Catch up my ass! If I find out…"

"Sis!"

She heard Kyndall's voice.

"Sis! Where are you?"

"In the closet."

Kyndall peered inside the room and headed into the spacious walk-in closet. "Julian let me in."

"I told Julian about letting people in my house."

"Girl, stop playing. What are you doing? Playing around in the closet?"

Leila pointed at the lipstick stain on Eric's shirt. "Look at this."

"Soooo…what are we doing here? I know you are NOT in the closet inspecting your faithful husband's clothes."

"I know I'm not trippin'. He's been acting strange lately. He said he had a client the other day, and when I got to the gym, he wasn't there."

"Well, what was his reasoning?"

"He said the client had a short session, and he went out to run some errands."

Kyndall looked at her sister like she was a little slow. "I mean...it doesn't sound far-fetched, Leila. I think you're overreacting." A sparkly dress caught Kyndall's eyes. "Oooo girl. When did you get this dress?"

"Really, Kyndall?"

"Can you blame me? I loooove this closet. It's so big. I'm going to need all this closet space when I get my home."

"I'm having a crisis, and you're looking around to see what you can steal from my closet."

"First, you're not having a crisis. Second, where is all this paranoia coming from? All the years I have known Eric, he has not even so much as looked in another woman's direction."

"All is know is he's been sneaking around here like he's up to no good, and maybe we're getting to that point in our marriage where my husband is getting bored."

"Have you sat down and talked to him?"

"I tried. He laughed at me, kissed me on the forehead, and walked out the door."

"And so now you're in the closet." Kyndall got distracted again. "Oooo, sis...when did you get these shoes? I might have to steal these for real!"

Leila shook her head, put the shirt back in the hamper, and exited the closet with her sister following behind.

Kyndall sat on the edge of the bed next to her sister. "Okay, sis. I see that you're really bothered, but seriously, Eric is not the type to be sneaking around with another female. He is a devoted husband and dad. That man loves the hell outta you. Whatever the spell was that you put on him, can I have the incantations?"

Leila couldn't help but laugh at her sister's remark. "You know you play too much. I'll sit down and try to have a decent conversation with my husband. Thanks sis. You may be right. It does seem out of character for him, but still—"

"No, we're not doing that. Stay positive. Enough about you, though. Can I tell you how my date ended?"

"Date? Is that what it was? I thought you were just having 'fun'," Leila gestured with air quotes.

"Stop being so technical. Anywhoo…remember Mark, the brother-in-law?"

"Yes, he actually had a conversation with Eric about going into the gym for some sessions."

"Well, let me tell you…he showed up at the bowling alley just as Teddy and I were leaving, and all hell broke loose."

Leila's eyes widened in anticipation. "What happened?"

Kyndall gave her sister the rundown from the beginning to the end, leaving her sister in disbelief and scratching her head.

"Wow! I wonder what that was about."

Shrugging, Kyndall agreed. "Me too. I still don't know the full story, and then, that's not the icing on the cake."

"More?"

"Yes. Devon had the nerve to show up at my place when I got home, he was posted up on the side of his car just waiting."

The concern was written all over Leila's face. "O no, K! I don't like that. Didn't you tell him it was over?"

"Yes! But he thinks just like all the other times that I'm going to change my mind."

Looking at her sister sideways, Leila had to question. "Are you?"

"No, I'm done done."

"Well, I hope you mean it, because you do deserve better." She patted her sister's knee. "Sounds like you had an eventful night."

"Very," Kyndall confirmed. "Sooo, let's do dinner tonight. I need some family time."

"You cooking?"

"No."

They both burst out in laughter.

Hours later at the neighborhood bar and grill, Kyndall was finishing up her second drink while Leila let the ice dilute hers.

"I don't know why you ordered that drink only for it to sit there and melt the ice," Kyndall questioned.

"Remember, you ordered the drink. I didn't even want it."

"Uhg...are you sure you're okay? You've been acting different."

"I don't know," Leila sighed. "My birthday's coming up. I think I'm going through a midlife crisis."

Kyndall almost choked on her drink from laughing. "Girl! Stop! Thirty-three and midlife crisis don't mix. Stop acting like an old maid."

"Then, maybe I'm hormonal."

"Per usual," Kyndall joked.

Something caught Leila's attention. "Speaking of hormonal, guess who just walked inside? Wow! What a coincidence."

"Who?" Kyndall looked back and saw Mark and his mom at the hostess stand waiting to be seated. "O my goodness! You know, he's very handsome, but he scares me."

Leila shooed her away. "He *is* a cutie but looks harmless, besides, he's with his mom. And thankfully, Teddy is nowhere in sight."

"Thank goodness. No telling what would happen if he were here."

The two sisters both watched intently as Mark and Cynthia were seated at a table across the restaurant.

"You think he saw us," Kyndall asked.

"I don't think so."

Mark pulled the chair out for his mom, and as his eyes scanned his surroundings, they landed on Kyndall, who was staring at him. His initial reaction was his natural attraction to her. He couldn't help but be enamored by her beauty, but then his emotions kicked in about the woman who was openly dating his sister's husband. To him, it didn't matter that his sister was missing. He didn't think it was right for Teddy to parade another woman around town; however, he couldn't fault her for Teddy's shortcomings and their ongoing feud. He and Teddy were never friends, and from the looks of it, would never be.

He sat down at his table but was obviously distracted.

"What's got your attention?" His mother asked, then looked in the same direction.

"Oh, I see. Now, I already had to bail you out of jail. Let's try not to catch another case. I swear, Mark. We have enough to deal with without you getting into more trouble. I'm sure Teddy is going to press forward with this case." Cynthia's increased frown lines signified her worry. "Lil Teddy will probably be a grown man before Teddy lets me see my grandson again."

Mark cupped his mother's hand in his. "I'm sorry, Ma. I'm going to make this right. If I have to remove myself out of the equation just so you can spend time with Lil Teddy, I will. But I don't think it'll come to that."

"Son, just leave well enough alone." She saw the wheels turning in his head, and it worried her even more. "I can't lose you too. Just stop. God is going to answer our prayers. We just have to have faith."

"Mom, I believe that, but we have to be proactive. Faith without works is dead. I know we're missing something. You heard Lil Teddy. Big Ted threw Monica's jacket away. The same fabric we found in the trail."

Cynthia didn't want to hear it. She shook her head repeatedly trying to shake the notion that perhaps Teddy was involved in Monica's disappearance.

"It's a lot to digest," she stated.

At that moment the waiter stopped by to take their orders. Afterwards, Mark dismissed himself from the table.

"I'll be right back, Mom."

"Mark...don't."

"I won't, Mom."

He walked over to Kyndall and Leila's table. Kyndall didn't know what to expect from him. His prior unpredictable nature had her on high alert.

"Hi, ladies," he greeted. "I know it's a little awkward and tense after what happened between me and Ted, but I want to apologize to you." He peered sincerely into Kyndall's eyes.

She nodded.

"I would like to clear the air and start fresh, if you let me. Would it be inappropriate to ask you to meet me for coffee one of these mornings?"

"I thank you for the apology, but I don't know if that would be a good idea."

"I promise you, it's not what you think," he pleaded.

She looked at Leila for help, but her sister lifted her eyebrows, shrugged her shoulders and left her hanging.

"Just coffee and conversation." Mark's sincerity along with his pleading eyes, gentle demeanor and Shemar Moore good looks made Kyndall's 'no' turn into a 'yes'.

"Thank you. I appreciate it."

Mark and Kyndall exchanged numbers and set up a coffee date. He then directed his attention to Leila.

"Tell your husband I'll be giving him a call to set up that session."

"I certainly will," she responded.

After he walked away, Leila quizzically looked at her sister. "Sis, what is going on with you? You tag along with me to a kiddie party and get yourself inserted between two men who hate each other."

"Your guess is as good as mine," she responded, then sipped her fruity beverage.

Mark strolled back to the table with his mom, and the smile on his face left her wondering.

"Son, what have you done?"

***

All was quiet when Leila arrived home. Julian was already in bed, and she assumed Eric was lounging after a long day at the gym. When she stepped inside the bedroom, he had his feet up and the television on; however, when he hurriedly ended his phone call as soon as he saw her, the alarm in her head went off again. Kyndall had done a good job of quieting her suspicions, but they had instantly returned.

He looked lovingly at his wife. "Come here, baby." He patted the bed. "How was your dinner date with Kyndall?"

She crept towards him, slipped out of her shoes, and sat her purse down.

"It was good. Who was that on the phone?"

"Oh, nobody. A client had a question."

"Oh." She sat down beside him.

"Baby, what's wrong," he asked.

"Nothing. Dealing with Kyndall's new drama."

"New drama? What's going on?"

Leila shook her head. "Where do I start? Do I start with the fact that her ex, Devon, did a stalker pop up at her place? Or do I start with the fact that she's dating, for lack of a better word, Teddy? Or do I start with that fact that Teddy's brother-in-law, Mark, was arrested after whooping Teddy's ass, *and* who so *happened* to be at the same restaurant tonight and invited Kyndall out for coffee?"

"Wow! That's a mouthful. What has your sister gotten herself into? But then again, I really don't care about all that right now. I just want to relax and spend some quality time with my beautiful wife."

Eric's words and the look in his eyes gave Leila a sense of security. She pushed aside her suspicions. *That's not the look of a man who's cheating,* she told herself. She took in the pajama pants he wore, his bare feet with the veins popping out of them, his bare chest that housed perfect muscles and the place where she loved to lay her head, his handsome face that she never got tired of looking at, which was looking back at her with a hint of mischief in his eyes.

She melted like butter on a hot skillet and cozied up to her man. She listened to his heartbeat while he lay back with his strong arms wrapped around her body. The intimacy of the moment led to deep caresses to passionate kisses to clothes piling on the floor to light then heavy moans to colorful fireworks exploding in the sky leaving its spectators in awe until the lovers fizzled out and drifted off to sleep in each other's arms.

The next morning Eric arose happy and refreshed. He looked down at his wife and smiled, delighted that he was able to ease whatever was on her mind last night. Seeing the restful way she slept, he didn't want to disturb her. He had an early morning client, so he rushed to the shower, hoping he didn't wake her.

Hearing Eric in the shower, Leila's eyes opened from her restful sleep. She turned around and saw her husband's phone on the night-stand. They had an amazing night, and she didn't want to taint it by starting the day with negative thoughts. However, she had to make sure there wasn't anything that she was missing. She never felt the need to violate his privacy, but she couldn't get rid of the nagging feeling. Whoever he was speaking to last night was quickly dismissed when she opened the door to the bedroom. She picked up the phone and looked at his call log.

"AW? Who the hell is that?" she asked herself.

She noticed the call lasted more than fifteen minutes and that AW was in the call logs a few more times. She wanted to jot down the number, but she heard the shower stop. She quickly put the phone back down and resumed her position in bed. Eric walked out the bathroom with the towel wrapped around his body.

"Hey beautiful. I didn't want to wake you up. You were looking so peaceful." He bent down and kissed her.

Leila's heart was beating out of her chest. She didn't know if she should question him or let it go. She didn't want him to know that she had looked through his phone.

"Hi, baby. You're up early," she said.

"Yes, I have an early workout session. What time are you coming in?"

"As soon as I drop Julian off to school."

When he finished dressing and walked out the door, she continued to lay in the bed and stare up at the ceiling. Deeply sighing, she thought, *am I imagining or is my husband really sneaking around? And why am I feeling like this all of a sudden?*

Coffee Talk

CHAPTER ELEVEN
COFFEE TALK

Kyndall walked into the coffee shop and saw Mark sitting at the table near the door. He looked calmer than the few times that she'd seen him before, but she was glad that she agreed to meet him in a public place. Maybe it was her curiosity or the inner counselor in her, but she didn't know why she agreed to the meeting in the first place.

Mark saw her and stood up to pull out the chair for her.

"Good morning. I told the server to take our order once you arrive."

"Good morning. Thank you so much," Kyndall responded.

There was an awkward pause as they looked at each other. Mark couldn't lie to himself. Her natural beauty had him at a temporary loss for words. Her red, glossy lips caught his attention while her beautiful browns stared back at him.

He finally broke the ice. "I know this is kind of awkward and a bit unconventional, but I feel like I have to explore all options, and you seem to be the best option that I have right now."

"Oh," she replied.

They were momentarily interrupted by the server, and after placing their coffee order, Kyndall continued.

"So, can you elaborate? What exactly are you needing from me?"

"First, I want to apologize again. I haven't been myself, and each time you've seen me, you were with Ted. Everything about that guy makes my skin crawl. I'm assuming you heard the story of my missing sister...Ted's wife."

Kyndall nodded.

"Ted has done little to nothing to help find her. It's like he's content that she's missing. And no offense to you, but he has the nerve to be openly dating, not only you, but another woman as well."

She was taken aback by Mark's revelation. Even though she only knew Teddy for a short amount of time, she didn't realize that he was seeing anyone.

Mark noticed the slight surprise in her eyes and kept speaking. "You're a beautiful woman and seem very nice. I don't want anyone else to get caught up in Ted's web. He and my sister were having some issues, and then she went missing. I've never been a fan of his. There was always something about him that didn't sit right with me. However, my sister was in love and blinded. When she started to see his true colors, she was already in too deep. The night I came to the bowling alley, my nephew had just revealed some vital information, and it sent me over the edge. I'm sorry you had to witness that."

She wondered what "vital information" did Lil Teddy reveal, and then she wondered how she had gotten herself entangled in their family dynamic. The server returned with their steaming hot coffee.

"Enjoy." She smiled and left the couple to resume their conversation.

"Oh, this smells so good." Kyndall closed her eyes as she took a whiff of the chocolate mocha coffee.

That simple act caused Mark to take pause and chuckle. He took in her charm and down-to-earth disposition. *Maybe I'm tackling this all wrong,* he thought. *She doesn't know me like that to owe me any loyalty.* He decided to reroute his delivery.

"They do make the best coffee here. This is my favorite," he said, holding up his caramel macchiato.

She noticed a genuine smile ease across his lips as well as the small dimple impressed on the top of his right cheek. It was endearing.

"So, I take it you come here often," she asked.

"Actually, I do." His smile faded. "Well…I did. My sister and I would meet here often to catch up."

"I'm truly sorry about your sister. That has to be horrifying to experience something like that."

"You have no idea," he nodded. "You and your sister…are you two close?"

Kyndall's face lit up. "Oh yes. We're best friends. Our parents made sure of it."

"Are your parents still around?"

"Yes. They retired and wanted to be close to the water, so they relocated to Clearwater."

"Oh, that's not far. I can tell they did an amazing job with you and your sister."

Kyndall's blush meter reached its peak. "Awww…thank you." She took a sip of her coffee.

"Actually, your sister and her husband were very nice to me. Eric gave me his card, and I told him that I'd contact him for a few workout sessions. I've been so busy with building my I.T. business and making sure my mother is good, that I've been slacking on my workouts. It's time to get back in the gym."

"Honestly, you look really good to me….uhm…" She stammered and tried to backtrack. "I meant that you look like you're always in the gym."

Kyndall's flustered expression made Mark laugh. "I know what you meant."

They talked endlessly for about thirty more minutes. He sat in admiration of the woman sitting across from him entertaining him of tales of her adolescent students that she counseled. *Who knew a whole sketch comedy could be made from the school counselor's desk?*

From the way he spoke about his family, Kyndall could tell that he was a family man and would do any and everything for them. She sympathized with him when he spoke of his father who had died after

Monica's disappearance. She almost shed a tear but held those emotions back. He had definitely tugged at her heartstrings.

"Not to change the subject, but what exactly is it that you think I can help with in regard to Teddy?" Kyndall asked.

Sighing heavily, Mark explained, "The day my sister went missing she wasn't supposed to go running. She and I were going to meet for coffee, but she never showed up. All I'm asking is if you see or hear anything out of the ordinary, please let me know. I know we just met, but I feel like I've run out of options. My mom and I are desperate for answers."

"First, let me say that I one-hundred percent empathize with this entire ordeal. It's been nice talking to you and getting to know a little bit about you, but I'm also in the beginning stages of getting to know Teddy and his son as well. I don't want to feel like I'm being deceitful or underhanded in any way. But with that being said, if…and I mean…if…I was to come across any information that could help you along the way, I'll be sure to convey it."

The fact that Kyndall didn't say no and was slightly willing to offer any type of assistance, gave Mark a grain of hope. He didn't have much hope to hang onto, but that simple agreement reignited the spark that he needed to continue to pursue answers to his sister's whereabouts.

"And that's all I can ask of you," he replied. "I know you don't owe any of us anything, but I do appreciate your time. You seem like a very caring and down-to-earth woman. I can see why Ted is smitten with you."

Kyndall was at a temporary loss for words. His last statement caught her off guard. Her bashful smile spoke for her.

"If I'm not asking too much, would you mind if we do this again?" he asked.

The uncertainty lingered in her head. "Uh…"

"Before you say no…just coffee."

She acquiesced. "Okay. I guess that's harmless enough. Why not?"

"Wonderful." He gave her an award-winning smile. "I know you have to get to work. Let me see you to your car."

Once inside her car, she thanked him again, then headed to work.

Interesting, she thought. *A kiddie birthday party turned into all of this.* Not normally one to immerse herself into drama, Kyndall found it odd that lately the drama was finding its way to her. Her mind began to wander. What IF Teddy had something to do with his wife's disappearance? She immediately shook that thought off. *No, I refuse to believe that.*

Once she got to work and settled at her desk, she looked through her calendar to confirm the sessions that she lined up for the day with some of her students. Her office phone rang on her desk.

"Good morning. Miss Rogers speaking."

The familiar voice quickly responded. "I have to call you on your office phone just to get a proper greeting?"

Irritated, Kyndall bit back. "Devon, please stop calling me."

"Wait, don't hang up. I just want to see you. I know I came off a little strong by coming to your place. I apologize. Can I take you out to lunch today?'"

"There is nothing more to talk about."

"Kyndall, I'm trying."

"Please don't. I'm so over it. Now, if you'll excuse me, I have work to do." With that, she hung up the phone, shaking her head.

"Unbelievable. He had all this, squandered it, and now he's trying harder to get me back than he did trying to keep me," she spoke into the atmosphere.

Her office phone rang again, and she hurriedly picked it up.

"Listen, Devon…I told—"

"Sis!"

Realizing that it was Leila calling, she calmed down. "I'm sorry, sis."

"I was calling to see how your coffee date went, but it seems like you got some other stuff going on."

"What else is new. Devon will NOT quit," she exasperatedly expressed.

"I'm starting to get a lil' worried about him."

"No need to worry, Leila. He'll get the picture soon enough. He's so used to me taking him back that he's having a hard time accepting that I'm done. He'll eventually stop. Besides, I'm sure he has more than enough to keep him occupied."

"He better, because one thing I don't play about is my sister!"

"I know you got my back. Anyway, I don't have a whole lot of time to talk, but my lil' coffee date, as you called it, was quite interesting. I'll tell you about it later. But before you go, just let me add that Mark's actually a nice guy...AND...he's easy on the eyes."

"OMG!" Leila couldn't believe her sister's audacity. "Why do I feel like you're digging yourself deeper into this thing?"

Finding it humorous, Kyndall replied, "I haven't had this much drama in my life in like forever. On one hand, it's kind of new and intriguing, and on the other hand, I keep asking myself do I really wanna open Pandora's box?" Interrupted by a knock on her office door, she quickly ended the conversation. "We'll talk about this later. I have a student at my door."

***

Teddy looked over at his son in the passenger seat who was not his usual self since being quizzed about his visit with Cynthia and Mark. When he phrased the questions to Lil Teddy, he tried to ask in a matter-of-fact manner so as not to make Lil Teddy think that he did anything wrong. The junior didn't indicate any wrongdoing on his part and rambled on about watching a movie, playing video games and eating cookies and popcorn. In his young mind, he was oblivious to the adult drama that surrounded him.

Teddy felt there was something that set Mark off for him to show up at the bowling alley in an uproar. Nevertheless, he planned to pursue pressing charges against his "brother-in-law". Mark was going to pay one way or another.

Breaking the silence, he informed his son, "Miss Kyndall will be coming by the house this evening to tutor you in your math. Make sure you bring all your homework assignments home."

"Okay, Dad. Is Miss Kyndall a math teacher?"

"No. She works at a school , but she's not a teacher. She's a counselor."

"What's that?"

"She talks to students who might need somebody to talk to and help them with their classes and grades."

"O...okay. There's Antonio!" Lil Teddy quickly dismissed his conversation with his father once he saw Yasmine and his friend, Antonio, in front of the school.

Teddy sighed. He was not in the mood to deal with Yasmine. He tried to get Lil Teddy out of the truck before she spotted him, but it was too late once Lil Teddy yelled his friend's name.

"Antonio!" he yelled as he jumped out of the truck.

The two boys greeted each other and ran into the school, leaving Yasmine to double back and head towards Teddy. He reluctantly let the window down when she approached.

"Good morning, stranger."

"Good morning," he dryly replied.

"Why do I feel like you've been dodging me?"

"Yasmine. Feel how you want to feel, but I've been very busy."

"I'm sure you've been busy. Busy with your new friend," she said, gesturing in air quotes.

"I'm not going to sit here and let you interrogate me."

She quickly changed her tone. "I'm sorry. I miss you. Can we do something tonight?"

"Tonight's not good. I'm still busy. I'll let you know when my calendar clears up."

Gasping, Yasmine responded, "Clear up? So, is that how this thing's going to go? Me begging and you pushing me to the side."

"This is not the time or the place," he stated.

At a loss for words, she simply replied, "Fine!" then huffed and puffed on her way back to her car. "Busy...yea...right. Okay, we'll see how busy you are when I just pop up again."

CHAPTER TWELVE
THE SESSION

After leaving work, Kyndall wanted to catch up with her sister, so she stopped by *Beast Mode*, and to her surprise, ran into Mark in the parking lot.

A bit taken aback by his presence, she expressed, "O wow! I didn't expect to see you here."

Mark gave her a reassuring smile. "It wasn't planned. I promise. Co-incidentally, Eric told me that this evening would be a good time to start my sessions with him. So, here I am."

"Nice. Not that you need the work." Her eyes did a once over.

Chuckling, he replied, "Maintenance...keeps me focused and in shape. Allow me," he said, opening the door.

"Thank you."

"Look what the cat drug in," Leila joked from behind the smoothie counter. "Hi Mark. Nice seeing you again. Eric said you were coming by for a consult. Let me get him."

"Thanks," he replied, then asked Kyndall, "Are you working out to-day?"

"Uh, no. I just stop by after work sometimes to harass my sister."

Finding her confession amusing, he laughed. "Ah. I see."

Just then, Eric appeared and greeted him with a handshake. "Hey, man. Glad you were able to come by."

"Thanks for the invite."

Eric motioned for him to follow him to the back, but before he left Kyndall's side, he asked, "Can I call you later?"

Caught off guard, she answered, "Uhm...sure. I'll be tutoring...uhm...I'll be free around nine."

Leila looked on with a raised eyebrow.

He smiled. "Great. Talk to you later." He left to join Eric.

Kyndall looked at her sister. "What?"

"Who are you, and what have you done with my little sister? First, Teddy, now, Mark, whoooo happens to be his brother-in-law. Lastly, we have Devon, who's still lurking around."

Kyndall groaned. "Please don't mention him."

"Is he still bothering you?"

"Yes!" she exasperatedly expressed. "He will NOT accept the fact that it's over."

"Do I need to call cousin, Pookie?"

Laughing out loud at her sister's reference to their imaginary cousin, Kyndall shook her head. "Not yet, but we may need to put him on speed dial just in case."

Leila leaned in closer to Kyndall. "So, tell me about your coffee date with Mark," she whispered so the men wouldn't overhear her.

"I didn't know what to expect at first, but surprisingly, he seemed like a good guy who deeply loves his family. There was a bit of a vibe, and you have to admit that he's easy on the eyes."

Leila shook her head. "So, what did he want?"

"That's the disturbing part. Without spelling it out letter by letter, he basically asked me to 'spy' on Teddy and let him know if I hear or see anything fishy."

Taken aback, Leila gasped. "Are you serious? This is getting messier by the day. And what did you say?"

"I simply told him that IF I did see anything, which I don't think that I will, I'll let him know."

"Sis, if Teddy found out, he'd be crushed. Even though I'm not totally sold on you getting involved with him at a time like this, I really think he likes you, and he'd be devastated if he found out that you went back reporting stuff to his estranged brother-in-law."

Kyndall thought the same thing. "I know. I actually have to go over there this evening to begin Lil Teddy's math tutoring. It kind of felt a little shady to be having a discussion about him with Mark."

Leila couldn't help but feel like her sister was getting in over her head, becoming too involved in Mark and Teddy's family drama. "You know what I think? You need to mind your business It's okay for you to date, but your current roster needs to be revamped. Teddy is technically married and has too much going on. Mark is too close to the situation. And Devon needs to tuck his tail between his legs and carry on."

Sighing and thinking about what her sister said, Kyndall let her know, "I understand your concerns, but we're here now, and I don't know if I want to just walk away."

"I think it's the counselor in you. But you can't fix everybody."

"I'm not trying to. I do want to be supportive, though."

"What am I going to do with you?"

"Make me a smoothie before I go, that's what."

Laughing out loud and shaking her head, Leila gathered the ingredients to whip up her sister's favorite smoothie.

An hour later, Teddy prepared spaghetti and garlic bread for dinner while Kyndall and Lil Teddy sat at the table practicing addition and subtraction of improper fractions. Kyndall's much-needed female presence was a welcome addition in their home. He noticed that Lil Teddy seemed to be at ease whenever she was around. He could see the extra effort his son put into making Kyndall proud.

Lil Teddy worked hard concentrating on her step-by-step instructions. Each time he got an answer correct, his face would light up. Kyndall's nurturing energy subconsciously reminded him of his mother. In the past, Monica had always been his greatest cheerleader and would constantly encourage him to do better.

"You're doing an amazing job, Lil Teddy. You'll be a professional math genius in no time," she complimented, beaming at him.

"Thanks, Miss Kyndall," he proudly stated.

"If you'd like to stay for dinner, I made extra," Teddy announced, hoping she wouldn't turn the offer down.

"It smells really good." She then turned to Lil Teddy. "What do you think? Should I stay and taste some of your dad's spaghetti?"

Lil Teddy's head bobbed up and down. "Yes! Dad makes the best spaghetti!"

She threw her hands up. "Well, I guess I'll be staying for dinner."

"Yay!" Lil Teddy exclaimed.

She gave him a wink and a playful pinch on the cheek.

Outside, Yasmine drove by Teddy's house.

"Yea, he's busy, alright," she stated out loud to herself, noticing the extra car in the driveway. "I know that's *her* car." She envisioned Teddy and Kyndall cozied up inside. "How can he just ignore me and let another woman claim my time?"

She was livid. She called Teddy's phone, and it went directly to voicemail. She tried again. Same result. She hit the steering wheel, then sent a text.

HOW COULD YOU! You can't just cast me aside and use me when you get ready! I've been more than patient. I'm not playing with you Teddy!!!

To her, Teddy was the love of her life who happened to have been in a loveless marriage with Monica. When word got out of Monica's disappearance, Yasmine secretly jumped for joy. Her competition was finally out of the picture.

I'll be damned if I let another woman step into the picture and take what's rightfully mine.

She almost got out of the car to bang on the door, but she wanted to see how long Kyndall stayed, so she remained patient.

"This is really good, Teddy," Kyndall stated after savoring the flavorful sauce that he whipped up with the spaghetti.

"Thanks. I aim to please."

"That you did."

"More wine?" he held the bottle towards her.

"No, thanks." This is more than enough. The only thing I'll be able to do when I get home is to climb into bed."

"I told you Dad makes the best spaghetti," Lil Teddy raved.

Kyndall giggled at Lil Teddy's critique. "And you told the truth!"

After dinner, Teddy cleared the table, and Kyndall felt obligated to help, but he would not hear of it.

"You've been more than helpful with my son."

"It's the least I can do."

Lil Teddy interjected. "Dad, can I show Miss Kyndall my new game before she leaves?"

"Son, I don't think we should bother Miss Kyndall. She has to get home."

"It's fine," she stated. "Yes, Lil Teddy, I would love to see your new game if it's okay with your dad."

"Pleeeeeze, Dad. It will only be for a minute."

Teddy wouldn't normally allow anyone to venture into his son's room, but a devilish smirk appeared on his face. He knew Monica would be watching.

"Sure, son, but only for a lil' bit. Miss Kyndall has to get home, and *you* have to get ready for bed."

Kyndall looked back at Teddy with a smile before she followed the junior to his room. He watched her sway and licked his lips. His desire to taunt Monica was the deciding factor in allowing his son to have company in his room. He had the monitors turned on and wanted Monica to see the latest competition.

Lil Teddy was excited to show off his newest and most prized gift, his gaming console and the latest games that accompanied it. His smile and energy were infectious, and Kyndall admired his youthful spirit. Despite his circumstances, he was a happy-go-lucky kid and well mannered. She humored him and engaged in his delight at showing and explaining his games to her.

Inside her prison, Monica sadly watched the strange woman interact with her son. *Another one of Ted's conquest*, she figured. Her heart broke and was at peace at the same time. Her beloved son looked happy in that moment. Whoever the woman was, Monica could tell that Lil Teddy liked her and vice versa. The woman was clearly beautiful, and the way she interacted with him seemed like she'd known him all his ten years. Monica didn't want to shed anymore tears; she had cried enough over the grueling, long months. But those fresh tears made an appearance as she watched her son, her baby, who had grown considerably since she last saw him up close and personal. *He looks so happy*, she sobbed. The sobs turned into wails. The pain was unbearable. She didn't know how much more she could take.

"I can't keep slowly dying! I can't!"

Teddy appeared in the doorway. "Ok, son. It's time for you to get cleaned up and ready for bed. Miss Kyndall has to get home. She's had a busy day."

"Thanks, Lil Teddy, for showing me your games. And you did a wonderful job on your math!" She gave him a high five and his face lit up.

"Thank you, Miss Kyndall. Good night."

Teddy guided her to the kitchen to gather her belongings. "I think he likes you," he mentioned.

"I like him too. He's a sweetheart."

"We Moore men aim to please."

"And that you do," she confirmed.

"Let me walk you to your car and see you off safely. It's a bunch of crazies roaming around."

"Such the gentleman."

He opened the front door and led her to the car. "Thank you so much for everything." He smiled down at her then leaned over to give her a kiss.

She accepted his lips, then his tongue. Her heart fluttered, her pulse raced, and just as quickly as it began, it ended. They momentarily gazed at one another. Each with a smile on their face.

She bashfully responded. "You're welcome, Teddy. I'm happy to help. I enjoyed the dinner as well."

"Anytime."

He opened the car door for her and waited until she pulled off. With his hands in his pockets, he stood on the side of the street until she turned the corner.

Parked a few houses down, Yasmine witnessed the exchange between Teddy and Kyndall and was beyond livid. She tried calling Teddy again before he got inside the house. She watched him look at his phone, shake his head, then forward the call to voice mail. She had the mind to run up inside the house, but when her phone rang, she thought maybe he had come to his senses. When she saw that the call was from her mother and not Teddy, she was once again deflated.

"Yes, Mom?" the aggravation evident in her tone.

"Meet me at the hospital! Antonio fell down the stairs. I think he broke his arm!"

"Oh no! I'm on the way!"

Her mission to ambush Teddy was put on hold as she drove off in both a fit of rage at Teddy and concern for her son. She vowed to return.

"He wants to replace me and ignore me like I'm just a random nobody! That's not gonna be so easy!"

Thee One

CHAPTER THIRTEEN
THEE ONE

"We gotta stop meeting like this." Kyndall smiled brightly as Mark pulled out the chair for her.

"Well, how else do you wanna meet? I'm liking this," Mark expressed. "Besides, now I know what kind of coffee you like, and I already ordered it."

She made the heart signal with her hands. Mark was charming and considerate once she tossed aside her initial perception of him. She tried to be objective even though she knew that his and Teddy's relationship was strained. Did she feel guilty meeting up with Mark knowing that both men were possibly interested in her? Slightly. Mark's plea and persistence won her over. Besides, she was no longer in a committed relationship and wanted to experience *all* that life had to offer.

He saw the twinkle in her eyes and wondered why she wasn't already taken. He was interested in her backstory. "Can I be a little more invasive this go round?"

"Hmmm...invasive? I guess that depends," she playfully replied.

Catching on to the innuendo, he smiled. "Nothing too serious. I was just wondering why there's no ring on that finger."

She looked down at her French-manicured hand, then back up at him. "Let's just say I have a habit of picking Mr. Wrongs."

"So, when Mr. Right comes along, are you open to one day being married and having kids?"

"Yes. Without a doubt. The only thing is, I'm not getting any younger and the pickins' are slim. I haven't been as lucky as my sister. She got a real one."

Mark laughed. "You still have time. Your Mr. Right is out there somewhere."

She playfully sighed heavily and exaggeratedly. "And what about you?" she asked.

"Honestly, I've been focused on my family these past couple of years. I haven't been able to think beyond that. I've been in a few long-term relationships over the years but haven't met *THEE ONE* yet," he explained in air quotes.

"Let's toast to Thee One."

They both raised their coffee cups, tapped them together and chanted, "To...Thee One!"

"Hopefully, that'll thrust our wishes out into the atmosphere."

"Fingers crossed."

They both laughed at the notion.

"Speaking of kids and family, have you happened to see my nephew?"

She was hesitant to answer. She didn't know if he would fly off the handle. She was still getting to know him and didn't want to set him off.

He sensed her hesitancy. "It's fine if you have. I just want to know that he's okay."

"Yes," she admitted. "Honestly, I'm doing a little tutoring with him. He was having some issues in math. I have another session with him later. Let me tell you, he's such a sweet little boy and very mannerable."

A proud but sad smile spread across his face. Kyndall noticed it immediately.

"If it's any consolation, I will tell him you asked about him," she stated.

He was hit with a bunch of emotions—sadness, anger, frustration. She questioned if she made the right decision by telling him.

"Thank you for letting me know. My sister used to quiz him on his math. It was their thing." He paused for a spell. "Can I ask you something?"

"Of course you can."

"I just want to make sure that what I tell you doesn't get back to Ted."

"Not only does my profession require me to be discreet, but so does my character. What we discuss is between us," she assured.

"When I showed up at the bowling alley the night you were with Ted, I had just found out from my nephew that Ted had thrown away a vital piece of evidence the day my sister went missing."

"Evidence?" She questioned in wide-eyed suspense.

"I don't want to say too much, but I feel like I need to let you know there was a reason for my actions."

"Mark, you can't just say that and not give more information."

He went on to explain to her what Lil Teddy had unknowingly revealed about the fishing outing and witnessing Ted throw away Monica's jacket.

"There has to be a good explanation," she tried to reason.

"I know you want to see the good in him," Mark said, shaking his head. "But he's not the squeaky clean man you think he is."

Not knowing how to respond to that, Kyndall let the thoughts of Teddy and Lil Teddy swirl through her head. *I can't imagine him being anything other than kind and upstanding. There's no way he could have anything to do with his wife missing as Mark is suggesting. No way.*

"I know it's a lot to digest, and I won't pressure you anymore with it, but, like I said, I wanted you to know why I acted a fool that night. I wanted to have a sit down with you and hope you won't hold it against me for future coffee dates." He lightened the mood with a smile.

She could get used to seeing him smile; it fit him so well, she thought, and she gave him one right back.

"You know how to put a girl on the spot, huh? I'm at a loss for words. You've just unloaded a lot, but I'm not going to leave you hanging. Coffee...sure...harmless...I think."

"Trust me. Coffee with me is harmless."

"I believe you," she said, looking at the time on her cellphone. "Can we finish this conversation later? I have to get to work."

"Sure thing," he confirmed, getting up to lead her out the door.

Later that day, Kyndall made her usual stop at the gym to talk with her sister. When she waltzed in and saw Eric standing over Mark as he did chest presses, she was momentarily in awe. The way he effortlessly handled the weight, turned her on. She wondered if he would be able to handle her the same way.

"Dang, sis. Do you need a cloth to wipe that drool from your mouth?"

Kyndall looked away from her distraction and shooed her sister away before adding, "I mean...do you see that? Who would've known that he could handle all that weight? He makes it look so easy."

Leila giggled at her sister. "Let me find out my lil' sister is crushing on the new man."

"Whatever. Is my smoothie ready? I gotta give you the latest."

"O Lord. Now what?"

Kyndall waited for Leila to sit the smoothie down before she commenced to tell her what Mark had revealed to her earlier.

With surprise and skepticism written on her face, Leila had to ask, "So, is he sure he heard Lil Teddy correctly? That's a big revelation. For him to say that Teddy got rid of Monica's jacket is implying that he had something to do with her disappearance. I just can't believe that."

Sucking up the fruity concoction, Kyndall shook her head. "Me either," she responded, coming up for air and getting a temporary brain freeze. "Oooo, sis. This is good. Did you add something new?"

Leila shook her head laughing. He sister could never stay on topic. "I added a lil' honey. Now, can you finish telling me the rest?"

"That's basically it. Mark thinks Teddy is involved, and he wants me to keep my eyes and ears open."

"This is getting too intense. You sure you want to be a part of all that? It's no secret that Teddy likes you. How do you think he'd feel if he knew you were plotting against him?"

"Whoa, sis. That's a tad overboard. Plotting?"

"You know what I mean. Not necessarily plotting but going behind his back and befriending his nemesis."

"OMG! You make it sound like a covert operation."

"It kinda is...maybe not on the secret spy level, but along those lines."

I like Teddy," Kyndall replied. "He's been nothing but a gentleman, and Lil Teddy is adorable. I couldn't imagine that man doing any harm to anyone, let alone his wife. I know there's bad blood between Mark and Teddy, and Mark's head is not clear when it comes to his brother-in-law. I don't know. It's complicated."

Leila threw her hands up and shook her head. "And you're supposed to be the counselor with all the answers."

They both found that statement humorous.

"Enough about me...are you done peeping through your husband's phone?"

Leila gestured with her finger against her lips. "Shhhh....geesh! Just say it out loud, why don't you. Let's just say I'm keeping my eyes wide open."

"Girl! You are wasting your time. The only woman Eric sees is you. Look at that handsome husband of yours.

They both looked over in the workout area and watched the two men interact with each other and unaware of the double pair of eyes feasting on them. Leila could only smile at her husband. Aside from Julian, Eric was her everything. The thought of him being disloyal gave her anxiety. She admired the way he took his time and catered to his clients' needs. He and Mark seemed to be bonding and working well together. Not only was Eric extremely attractive on the outside—the handsome face, the supple skin, the body of a god—he was just as attractive on the inside. Leila knew she struck gold when she met and married her Prince Charming. If only she could get those nagging feelings out of her head, she thought.

After minutes of mindless chitchat, the women were pleasantly interrupted by Eric and Mark, who had just concluded their session.

"I saw ya'll checking us out," Eric teased.

Mark's and Kyndall's eyes met. He grinned while she blushed. The married couple caught the apparent undeniable attraction between the two, and Eric winked at his wife, signifying what they both witnessed.

"Don't flatter yourselves. We were just watching you do your thing. That's all," Leila teased back. "Mark, would you like a smoothie?"

"No, thanks. I actually have to get going," he replied, then he looked over at Kyndall. "Later?" He asked, hoping that they could continue their conversation.

She took a quick survey of his appearance—the sweat towel hung loosely around his neck, his light skin glistened from the workout sweat, and the wetness of his low-cut, curly hair gave him an innocent, boyish charm. She tried to appear nonchalant, but her heart skipped a beat and she just knew a schoolgirl crush had developed.

"Uhm...sure. Call me," she said.

He gave her a nod and a gigantic smile before turning to Eric. "See you in a couple days, brother."

They both dapped, then Mark exited the building feeling exhilarated; a feeling he hadn't felt in a long time.

Once he was gone, Leila spoke first. "OMG, sis!"

Kyndall raised her hands, "What?"

"I saw you blushing."

"Don't be too hard on her," Eric stated before giving his wife a kiss. "I like Mark. He gives good vibes. I haven't known him for long, but I can tell he's solid. He gets my stamp of approval, if that's saying anything."

Kyndall's face lit up. "Really? I've never heard you speak that highly of anyone before."

He shrugged. "I mean...you know I love you, sis, but you haven't always made the wisest choices when it came to men. But that's not my business. I just want you to know that Mark's a good dude." He patted her on the shoulder and walked away, leaving the two women surprised by his confirmation.

***

Cynthia watched while Mark stood at the kitchen counter cutting up fruit. He was humming a tune she was not familiar with. She walked over to him and stared for a few seconds.

"Yes, Ma? You want some?"

"It does look good, but no. I was just checking you out. I noticed you seem a bit cheery these past few days."

"Cheery? Is that your word for it?"

They both giggled.

"Yes. Cheery," she confirmed. "Does this new attitude have anything to do with that pretty woman?"

He paused for a spell while a smirk magically appeared on his lips. He couldn't help but smile thinking about Kyndall. Somehow, their conversations and their brief interactions left him feeling high-spirited. He couldn't remember the last time he felt that way. Aside from her obvious beauty, there was something about her that he liked. It was hard for him to contain. He didn't have to answer his mother's question. His reaction said it all.

Although she was happy her son was in good spirits, she didn't know if he was making a wise decision by dealing with someone who was obviously somehow involved with Teddy. From what she could tell at the party, Teddy and Kyndall seemed quite chummy.

She rubbed her son on the back and let her last words marinate before she said what was on her mind. "You don't have to answer that. It's written all over your face." She then changed the course of the conversation. "I know you're feeling good right now, and I hate to rain on your parade, but we need to talk about you and these pending charges."

He groaned.

"I think you need to suck it up and apologize to Big Ted. Perhaps he will drop the charges and allow Lil Teddy to come back again."

His mother sure knew how to ruin a mood, he thought. "Ma, do you really think I'm going to stand in Big Ted's face and actually apologize? He's lucky that that's all I did to him. It could have been worse. I want to see Lil Teddy just as much as you do, but we just have to let this thing play out. I truly believe that something is about to happen. I don't know what, but I feel it in my bones."

Uninvited Guests

CHAPTER FOURTEEN
UNINVITED GUESTS

"Guess what, Miss Kyndall?"

Kyndall giggled at Lil Teddy's eagerness to spill whatever news that he was holding onto. "Hmmm...tell me."

"My friend, Antonio, is having a sleepover on Saturday."

"O, really? That sounds like fun."

"I can't wait. He broke his arm, so his mom is letting him have friends over because he was sad."

"You're a good friend, then, Lil Teddy...helping to cheer him up."

While Teddy put the finishing touches on dinner, he listened to Kyndall and Lil Teddy's conversation at the table during his tutoring session. He inwardly sighed when his junior mentioned Yasmine's son, Antonio. Since meeting Kyndall, Teddy had been putting Yasmine on the backburner. He no longer wanted to deal with her antics and her neediness. The single and the beautiful, Kyndall, had caught his attention, and he was laser focused on trying to take their newfound friendship to the next level. However, Lil Teddy begged him to attend Antonio's sleepover, so he reluctantly agreed.

"You're also a good learner," Kyndall added. "You've answered all of these questions correctly." She held her hand up and gave Lil Teddy a high five.

"Good job, son," Teddy said, fixing a plate of baked potatoes, green beans and baked chicken. "Kyndall, are you staying for dinner?"

"I need to get home early this evening. I have a lot of things on my to-do list that need my attention."

Her phone buzzed with a text. She quickly looked at it and a noticeable smile swept across her lips. The way she smiled, Teddy could tell that whoever it was, was someone special. He subconsciously felt a wave of jealousy. When she put her phone down and looked up at him, she thought she caught a glimpse of him peering at her, then his facial expression instantly changed.

"I can make you a plate to go," he told her.

"Teddy, you're so nice."

"Please eat dinner with us," Lil Teddy pleaded.

She didn't have the heart to tell him no. They were both looking at her with expectant eyes.

"Okay," she relented. "I guess I can stay for a lil' while and fill up my belly." She smiled and rubbed her flat stomach.

Lil Teddy's smile made her weak. Once again, she found herself engaging in chitchat and dinner with Teddy and his son. When her phone buzzed again with another text, she caught Teddy's eyes once more and couldn't decipher if it was jealousy or insecurity or maybe both. It made her think of all the things that Mark said about him. She decided to wait to check the message just to be on the safe side of his emotions. It had become obvious that he was watching. Once they were done eating, and Lil Teddy ran off to his room, she thanked Teddy for the meal and offered to wash the dishes, which he refused.

"Teddy, it's the least I can do. The food was great, and I would feel bad about leaving you behind to clean up." She grabbed the plate from his hand, grazing it in the process. After she bent down and put it in the dishwasher, he grabbed her hand and turned her to face him.

"Believe me," he said. "I appreciate you tutoring my son. I think he likes you. A lot. So, having you stay behind and eat dinner with us is our pleasure. Remember that." His light brown eyes bore into her soul while his head slowly moved closer to her lips, but before he could seal the deal, the doorbell rang.

"Saved by the bell...literally," Kyndall teased. "I'll finish the dishes while you go answer the door."

He wasn't expecting company, so he had a puzzled look on his face. "Let me get rid of whoever this is. I'll be back."

He marched to the door, mumbling underneath his breath and ready to cuss out whoever it was that interrupted his precious moment with Kyndall. The doorbell rang once again, then again. He angrily snatched the door open without looking through the window to see who it was. Yasmine stood on the other side with her arms folded and an angry scowl on her face.

"You actually answered the door? I figured you'd be laid up with that BITCH by now!" she snapped.

Teddy was irate. The nerve of Yasmine to pop up at his house unannounced, causing a disturbance. He stepped outside, closing the door behind him.

"How dare you?" He didn't raise his voice, but the sinister, even-toned bass of his voice, along with the coldness in his eyes, sent shivers down her spine.

Inside, Kyndall continued to help with the dishes, but the word "bitch" caught her attention. Normally one to mind her business, her curiosity got the best of her as she slowly and carefully walked to the front door. She heard voices but couldn't make out what was being said. She peeked out the window and saw Teddy and the woman, Yasmine, having an obviously heated discussion. She leaned in closer to the door to hear better, and her eyes bulged when she heard Yasmine say, "All the years I've waited for Monica to be out of the picture, so we could live our happily ever after, and now you're acting different by playing in my face with another woman. She aint even that cute."

Kyndall's head snapped back. She rolled her eyes and wanted to go out and confront Yasmine. *I beg her pardon. She don't even know me like that!*

"Jealousy is not attractive on you. Know your place," she heard Teddy say. "Leave now, Yasmine, or you WILL regret it."

Kyndall couldn't believe that the voice belonged to the same sweet Teddy that she had come to know. She was taken aback hearing that side to him.

She heard Yasmine respond. "Everything I've done for you, and this is how you treat me!"

"Yas, go home...NOW!"

Kyndall didn't hear a rebuttal, so she figured Yasmine obeyed his command. The next thing she heard was a car start. She rushed back to the kitchen, pretending that she didn't hear all that she did. When Teddy nonchalantly walked back in with a fake smile on his face, she was wiping the table. *I know he didn't just walk back in here like he didn't just have an argument with his mistress.*

"Company?' she asked.

"No, that was just my neighbor asking for a favor."

His blatant lie left her flabbergasted. The impending awkward moment was saved when Lil Teddy rambunctiously appeared from his room.

"Miss Kyndall, can you read this book with me before my bedtime?"

"Son, we can't keep Miss Kyndall all night (*I wish I could*). She has to get home."

The disappointment in Lil Teddy's eyes made her agree to his wishes. "I can stay for a teeny while longer. What book are you reading?"

"It's about a little boy who dreams of building a spaceship so he can take his classmates up to space."

"Oh...sounds interesting." She looked at Teddy with understanding in her eyes. "You mind?"

He gave her the greenlight, and she ended up sitting on the chair next to Teddy's bed while he got cozy underneath the covers as she began to read a chapter from his book. Little did she know, her presence in the house reminded Lil Teddy of his mother. On top of helping him at the dinner table with his math, Monica used to read to him at night before bed. In his mind, it was like having his mother back again, and he didn't want to let that feeling go. Kyndall even imitated the different voices and sounds like his mother did, which made him laugh out loud. Kyndall laughed along with him when she got to the funny parts.

Monica quietly lay in her prison and watched the monitor overhead. She witnessed the interaction between her son and the woman again. Seeing the joy on her son's face caused her not to be bitter towards the woman. Whoever she was, she could tell that Lil Teddy adored her and vice versa. It was evident in their seemingly authentic communication with one another.

It broke her heart to see her son giving another woman the same look he used to give her, but on the other hand, it soothed her soul to see that her son was just fine and not suffering from her disappearance. Knowing that Lil Teddy was thriving and happy was the only thing that she cared about at the moment. It made her decision to finally end it all that much easier.

***

On the drive home, Kyndall reflected on everything that had transpired in the past weeks. Everything that Mark said about Teddy started flooding her brain. *Was there some truth to some of the things he said?* Hearing the coldness in which he spoke to Yasmine, although well deserved, was new to her. Prior to that, she had not witnessed that side to Teddy, and it took her for a loop. She didn't know how to feel about him lying to her about his uninvited guest and was happy that Lil Teddy had interrupted at that moment in time, because she didn't know if she would have been able to maintain a poker face. She didn't want to give away the fact that she had been eavesdropping on his confrontational conversation.

The kiss that Teddy gave her before she left his house was awkward. She could tell that he wanted more, but with the recent revelations about his character, she found herself becoming cautious. To see him in a new light, brought about a queasy feeling. *Is he really that cold and heartless? Is it all a façade?* She then recalled the text message that she left unread because of the look on Teddy's face. That was another red flag.

His fleeting facial expression was a subtle warning sign that she couldn't ignore.

When she got to the traffic light, she finally looked at the message. It was from Mark.

Morning coffee? (a piping, hot-coffee emoji and praying hands)

The simplicity of the message brought about a big grin followed by a quick reply.

Sure! (a happy-face emoji)

The traffic light turned green, and she proceeded along her route home, unaware of the car trailing her.

***

"If this Bitch thinks she can come in between what I've built with Teddy over the years, then she is sadly mistaken." Yasmine was beyond furious. Teddy had treated her like an afterthought and sent her on her way like a stray dog only to replace her with Kyndall. Yasmine was not going to be outdone. She needed to know who this woman really was, and her first priority was to find out where she lived. Instead of leaving Teddy's house like he demanded, she stayed behind to find out how long Kyndall stayed and to follow her after she eventually left.

When Kyndall pulled into the driveway of her townhome, Yasmine slowly crept by so she could make a u-turn and double back without being noticed. She stayed a comfortable distance away from Kyndall's place with her lights turned off, then saw a pregnant woman approach Kyndall while she exited her car. She wished she could hear the conversation, because it looked like they were in a debate—the hand gestures, the neck rolls, the finger pointing, and the head shakes.

"Looks like drama." Yasmine grinned. Misery loved company. Now that she had a leg up on this Kyndall woman, she decided to leave, but she definitely had plans to make her presence known when the time presented itself.

Weekend Plans

CHAPTER FIFTEEN
WEEKEND PLANS

Friday morning

Kyndall walked into the coffee shop like a zombie. Mark could tell that she had a rough night. Her eyes were puffy like she'd been crying, her hair was tied back in a ponytail, and there was no pep in her usual sway. He quickly got up and pulled the chair out.

"Make mine a double," she joked, sitting down with a serious look on her face.

He passed her the cup of coffee that he already had waiting for her.

"Take a couple sips, then let me know how I can help." With genuine concern, his brown eyes met her serious gaze.

She wrapped her hands around the cup of hot deliciousness, blankly stared at him, then heavily sighed. She contemplated whether or not she wanted to discuss her personal business with him, even though she was in some way involved in *his* business. She watched how patiently he waited for her to speak, and then, as if reading her indecisive mind, he took her hand and gently rubbed the top of it with his thumb, looking into her eyes.

"You can trust me."

The sincerity in his eyes, his voice, and his touch not only sent minor shock waves through her body but gave her the confirmation she needed. She sighed once more, then told him how her night ended.

"When I got home last night, I had a visitor waiting outside."

His eyebrows furrowed. He didn't like the sound of that, but he didn't interrupt.

"A pregnant woman," she continued.

Then his eyebrows raised, curiosity setting in.

"Yes," she nodded. "A pregnant woman whom I never met a day in my life. Not only did she know where I lived, she came in hot...accusing me of sleeping with her man."

His eyes widened, wondering of the possibility. "Did you?" he asked.

"Apparently, I was...only I didn't know it. I guess you can say I was sleeping with *both* our man. I'd really like to wring Devon's neck right now." She mocked strangling someone.

Mark saw the anger and hurt in her eyes.

"I dated this man for two years and had no clue whatsoever that he had a whole nother household and a whole nother woman. I knew he was a serial cheater...that's why I left, but I left because of the women that I *knew* about. *This* one was a total shocker. They have a one-year old and another on the way. He knew how much I wanted a family, and he did this to me! I'm so mad right now I could scream!" She tried not to raise her voice.

Mark's angry facial expression matched hers.

"So, how did she find you?"

"Can you believe this? She hacked his emails and saw an old receipt for some flowers he sent me during one of our many breakups. She also saw pictures of me along with some of the other women he'd been dating. No offense, but men can be so stupid. I really shouldn't be surprised, but the pregnancy took me for a loop."

"Kyndall, I'm sorry. Believe me, if that's the kind of man he is, then he didn't deserve you. He doesn't deserve *any* woman. A man who does that has a lot of soul searching to do. Don't let that loser take away from the amazing woman you are."

She tilted her head and looked at him with fresh eyes. She allowed his words to calm her resolve.

"Thank you for that. Behind all that toughness is a very sweet gentleman," she told him, and thought she saw a hint of bashfulness.

"I'm speaking facts. He's not your problem anymore. You did what you were supposed to do...leave and move on."

"Thankfully, but he has another thing coming. He's constantly calling, texting and begging me to meet up with him so he can plead his case for me to take him back. The audacity, huh?"

Mark shook his head. "You're kidding?"

"No. Look." She showed him the long list of text messages from Devon. "He even sent this one last night after I got the visit from his pregnant girlfriend/fiancé/ baby mama, or whatever."

"Unbelievable."

"That's fine, because after I got Vanessa, (that's her name), to calm down and see that I was just as much in the dark as she was, we decided to catch his ass in the act. She agreed to keep quiet until she gets confirmation from me. I'm sure he'll be calling as usual, so guess what?"

Mark understood what their next play was going to be. "You don't even have to finish. I already know how this is supposed to play out. Do you need me to hang around as backup?"

"That might not be a bad idea, actually."

"Say no more. I only hope that you realize that you're the prize, and he doesn't deserve any more of your good energy."

She breathed in deeply, letting his kind words sink in. "I appreciate you saying that, and believe you me, as soon as this is over, I've totally washed my hands of him, even if I have to get a restraining order."

"I hope it doesn't come to that, but you have to do what you have to do for your own peace of mind."

They both sipped on their coffee in unison, then Kyndall sat back in the chair and let the tension drain from her body.

"Wow," she expressed. "Sitting here talking to you about this has been unexpectedly therapeutic."

Smiling, Mark replied, "I'm happy I could assist. Considering all the heavy stuff I put in your ear already, that's the least I could do."

She wanted to tell him about Yasmine's pop-up appearance at Teddy's house, but she didn't have the energy or the nerve to bring it up. She decided to hold on to that for another day. She'd already given him an earful of enough drama for the day, and it was still early. She didn't feel like contributing to him flipping his lid hearing about Teddy's drama.

She looked at the time on her phone. "I have to get going...work calls, but I do want to continue our conversation. There's something else I want to tell you."

He was elated that she wanted to meet again, but he was questioning what that something else was. His antennas went up, but he kept his cool.

"Sure," he replied.

"I'm meeting my sister and Eric Saturday evening for dinner. Why don't you join us?"

'That's an invite I wouldn't turn down," he said.

Just as she got up to leave, her phone buzzed with a text from Devon.

"Well, well, well...look who we have here," she smirked, thinking about putting an end to his scandalous ways.

***

"Thanks, Mom, for keeping Lil Teddy this weekend. I have a lot of stuff to take care of. He was going to go to his friend Antonio's sleepover, but I decided that it's best he spend the weekend with you instead," Teddy said, while he and his mother were seated in the backyard waiting for Lil Teddy to pack his bookbag.

"You know it's no problem," Felisha responded. "I love spending time with my grandson. I have a list of fun things that we're going to do." She added, "You *do know* that Cynthia would help take some of the burden off of you if you'd let her. She loves him too, Teddy."

Exasperated, he looked at his mother. "Not now, Mom. It's not so much Cynthia as it is Mark, but both of them irk the hell outta me. I'm not their favorite person and the feeling is mutual, especially right now. Mark's definitely on my hit list."

"Maybe you should have a conversation with Cynthia and you two could come to some sort of supervised visitation without Mark until all of this nonsense dies down."

"Mom, I said my peace. Discussion is over," he got up and went inside the house.

She knew talking to her son about Mark was fruitless, but she tried to do her part to bring the family together for the sake of Lil Teddy. She and Cynthia were never the best of friends due to their different personalities; however, as a mother, she empathized with her. Cynthia didn't deserve to be left out of their grandson's life; she'd already lost her daughter and her husband. Right was right, and wrong was wrong, and she didn't have a problem expressing that to Teddy. He was being unreasonable. That is why Felisha decided to take matters into her own hands. What Teddy didn't know wouldn't hurt, and it would make all the difference in Lil Teddy's and Cynthia's life.

***

Saturday afternoon

"What's that new scent I smell?" Cynthia grinned at her son who was standing in the bathroom mirror after splashing some aftershave on his bright, smooth skin. She noticed that he'd been in an unusually good mood recently, and she loved the change. It reminded her of the old Mark, before Monica's disappearance.

"Do you really wanna know or are you fishing for something else?"

She reached in front of him and picked up the bottle. "Oh...Midnight Dream." She teased him, reading the name of the product. She put the bottle back down on the sink, and her smile never left her eyes. "I'm happy to see you in a good mood. Where are you going?"

"I'm going to meet a few people at the restaurant on the strip."

"Oh...nice. Welllll....guess who I'm going to meet up with this evening?"

He was stumped by his mother's question. He didn't think his mother was dating, and if she was, he didn't know how he would feel about it. He'd only known her to be with his father and wasn't ready to see her dating anyone. On top of everything else that was going on in their lives, it was too soon.

"Who?" he seriously asked with an air of protection.

"Lil Teddy."

Mark was puzzled. "Lil Teddy? You mean to tell me that you were able to convince that idiot to let you see your own grandson?"

"No," she shook her head. "You were right. Big Ted's a lost cause. You won't believe that Felisha reached out to me and said she was taking Lil Teddy to the arcade today. She asked if I'd like to meet them there. Of course, she didn't run it by Ted, but that's between us."

He was surprised and impressed by Felisha's gumption. "You sure it's not a trap? I don't trust Big Ted *or* his mama."

"What would she have to gain from trying to trap me?"

He shrugged. "I don't know, but why now, all of a sudden? Why don't you tell her to meet you at the arcade that's on the strip next to the restaurant? That way I can come by and see my nephew and keep an eye out at the same time, just in case."

"I'll see if Felisha will agree." She shook her head. "You're always so leery of everyone."

"Not everyone, Ma. I just want to make sure you're safe. I don't trust Ted or anyone associated with him."

"O really? Then why are you chasing behind that woman?"

He was temporarily muted. "That's different," he sheepishly replied, not wanting to continue that conversation with his mother because he found himself liking Kyndall more and more each time he saw her. He just wasn't ready to acknowledge that fun fact or say it out loud.

"Sure. Okay son." Cynthia laughed and walked away.

Mark was looking forward to spending more time with Kyndall. He liked her vibe; she was fun, beautiful, and they had good conversations. Her invitation to hang out with her, Eric and Leila was surprisingly un-expected, and he was going to take full advantage of it. He didn't ex-pect to have to deal with his mother's meetup with Felisha, though. He would be beside himself if something happened to Cynthia. She seemed so happy talking about Lil Teddy, and he didn't want to dampen her happy mood. He'd just have to play double duty and keep an eye out on Cynthia while entertaining Kyndall. He didn't trust Felisha as far as he could see her.

***

Yasmine vowed to take Kyndall out of the picture and off of Teddy's mind. Teddy's interest had shifted, and Yasmine was not satisfied with sitting in the background while he entertained someone else. As she inconspicuously sat outside Kyndall's place, she was ready to execute her plan for the evening. Yasmine had to get Teddy alone, but she needed to make sure that Kyndall and Lil Teddy would not be a hindrance. Teddy had already informed her that Lil Teddy would not be at the sleepover and was going to spend the weekend with his grandmother, Felisha. That took care of Lil Teddy. Kyndall, however, was a wild card, and needed to be monitored.

Once she saw Kyndall get into her car and drive off, Yasmine secretly tailed her once again. "I had Teddy first," she spoke out loud to herself. "I'm not going to play nice and let you sink your teeth into my man!"

Yasmine had a lot of parking options when Kyndall pulled into the shopping plaza that housed a host of restaurants, boutiques, a movie theater and arcade. She watched from afar as Kyndall got out and strolled to the Japanese restaurant. Yasmine enviously turned up her nose at the woman's toned, brown legs underneath the short, lavender romper she wore, commanding attention with the matching wedges. Her pressed hair with the part down the middle slightly swung with every step she took. Yasmine hated to admit that the woman was definitely competition in more ways than one.

When she saw Monica's brother, Mark, meeting with Kyndall at the entrance of the restaurant with a huge grin on his face, she had to do a double take. "I know that's not Mark?" She squinted her eyes at the two of them, and when they gave each other a hug, she gasped and pulled out her phone. "What's really going on?" She tried to get a picture, but they had already gone inside.

"O hell no! What are those two up to?" She was privy to the tumultuous history between Mark and Teddy, and it seemed to her that Kyndall's interest in Teddy *and* Mark was a conflict of interest that didn't sit well with her. She debated with herself whether or not she wanted to go inside. A picture was worth a million words that would work in her favor; she needed to show Teddy that his new prospect was not so loyal.

Before going inside the restaurant, she tried to disguise her appearance by teasing out her hair to partially conceal her face, then she put on some shades. *Hopefully, no one will recognize me*, she thought. She went inside and told the hostess that she'd sit at the bar. As she made her way to the corner of the bar, she scanned the restaurant to see if she could spot them. After carefully scanning each section of the restaurant, she finally spotted the couple along with Eric and Leila. They were all engaging in conversation around the hibachi grill.

When did this quartet happen? She pulled out her phone and snapped a few pictures. *This bitch thinks she can cozy up to my man AND his brother in law! I don't think so, honey.* Satisfied with her solid evidence, she got up to leave, but before she did, she took a long lustful stare at Eric. *Uhm uhm uhm...too bad he's a one woman man.* She then quickly walked out before they saw her. Once she got in her car, she was breathing hard and was in disbelief that Kyndall had the audacity to interrupt the flow of things between her and Teddy only to be gallivanting around the city with Mark too. *NOT ON MY WATCH!*

As she headed out of the parking lot, she saw Lil Teddy with his grandmother, Felisha, and they were walking towards the arcade.

"Goodness. What's going on this evening? I need to stop and speak to Miss Felisha and Lil Teddy," she said to herself. But when she saw Lil Teddy running towards the door and hug his maternal grandmother, Cynthia, who was sitting on the bench outside the entrance, Yasmine was baffled. She was aware of the feud between the two families and thought it was odd that Felisha and Cynthia were meeting up.

"Hmmm...maybe I won't go say hi after all." She took that moment to snap another picture with her phone. Lil Teddy looked happy and the two women looked to be the best of friends who were catching up. "Once I get my man back acting right, I can show these to him. He might need to know what's going on if he doesn't already."

Armed with an arsenal of damaging photos, Yasmine texted her mother that she'd be gone the rest of the evening and to kiss Antonio good night, then she set off on her next mission: REMIND MY MAN WHO TF I AM!

Saturday Date Night

CHAPTER SIXTEEN
SATURDAY DATE NIGHT

The intense heat from the large flame waved in their direction as the foursome sat around the hibachi grill, enjoying the showmanship of the talented chef. The flame quickly died, and Kyndall turned to Mark.

"Do I still have eyebrows left?" she asked, laughing.

Mark did a quick inventory of her facial hair and gave her the thumbs up. "Yes, they're both still intact."

They all laughed.

"Mark, I'm glad that you could join us, man." Eric said.

"Thanks for the invite," he looked at Kyndall. "I haven't been to one of these in years. Me and my sister..."

Kyndall put her hand on his knee to let him know that it was okay, and he didn't have to further explain.

"Brings back good memories," he finished with a smile. Kyndall's hand had sparked something in him. "So...is this date night *or* a night out with friends? I can call you all that, can I? Friends?"

"This is *our* date night," Leila answered, cozying up to Eric. "Julian is at his uncle's house with his cousins, and we're enjoying grown people time. Sis, are you and Mark on a date?" she teased.

"Why're you trying to put me on the spot," Kyndall asked. "I would like to say that I'm on a date with someone that I'm getting to know better. We're on a friendly date. How about that?"

Mark grinned. "I'll toast to that."

They all laughed and lifted their cocktails. In unison, they said, "Cheers!"

"Since we got that out of the way, I need to tell you this," Kyndall said, looking at her sister and Eric. "I had a very unexpected visitor show up at my house."

"Who?"

Kyndall told them the same story she told Mark about Devon's girl-friend/fiancé/baby mama showing up to her place and confronting her. Leila was fit to be tied.

"I know you're joking, right?"

"Nope." Kyndall shook her head. "But that's fine, because we'll have the last laugh, and then I'm one hundred percent done with his stalking ass."

"And how do you plan on doing that?"

Kyndall gave her sister all the juicy details of how she was going to deal with Deceitful Devon. Leila was not too keen on Kyndall taking on Devon and thought that she should leave well enough alone, but after hearing the plan, she couldn't help but be entertained by the notion.

"Oh, that sounds like I need a front row seat. But what if he gets outta hand?" Leila asked.

Mark didn't hesitate to respond. "That's where I come in."

The chivalrous gesture got a rise out of Kyndall. All bright thirty-two's showed. "Yes, he's going to accompany me."

Leila and Eric shared a look.

"What?" Kyndall asked, even though she knew what their look suggested. "Mark already knew what went down between me and the baby mama. He was the first person I saw after it happened, so we discussed it."

"You two are getting mighty cozy." Leila couldn't help teasing her sister.

"Are you jealous that Kyndall has someone else to tell all her problems to except you?" Eric joined in the playful banter to take the heat off Mark and Kyndall.

"Be quiet," Leila playfully shoved his arm. "You're supposed to be on my side."

At that moment, Eric's phone buzzed in his pocket, but he ignored it. Leila felt the vibration as well and wondered if he was going to check it. He didn't. She made a mental note of it.

The conversation amongst the four of them continued to flow while they watched the chef use his culinary instruments to flip, toss, chop, and dice up their food with a comedic flair. As he plated their selected dishes and sat each plate before them, Eric excused himself from the group to go to the restroom. Leila's antennas went up. She just knew he was going to take that time to check his phone. *What is he hiding? Or better question, who is he hiding?*

When he returned, she didn't know if the smile on his face was for her or the person who was on his phone. She squinted her eyes at him, and he sat down comfortably and kissed her on the cheek. *Was that a guilty kiss or a genuine kiss?* She wondered to herself. It wasn't unusual for him to kiss her on the cheek or show affection; it was something he always did. She hated that she had to question his intentions and decided at that moment not to dwell on it. They were all having a decent time drinking, eating and enjoying each other's company. Kyndall was in her element with Mark, and it was refreshing to see her having a good time with someone who seemed to be deserving of her time. Leila was going to dig deeper later to find out why her husband had recently taken to acting secretive.

Kyndall's next topic of conversation had them all glued to their seats. "I don't know if I should say this or not, but Teddy had a visitor when I was there tutoring Lil Teddy." She looked at Mark. "I know you asked for full transparency, and I don't want to get any drama started, but it kind of made me see Teddy in a different light."

Mark held his tongue, not wanting to disrupt what she was saying. Nothing about Teddy surprised him anymore. He knew the type of man Teddy was, and eventually, given enough time, everyone associated with the monster would see his true colors. Eric and Leila sat in anticipation of Kyndall's story.

"Yasmine showed up unannounced. I was in the kitchen, so I didn't know that it was her at the door until I heard loud talking and cussing. I went to eavesdrop at the door and couldn't believe the things they said to each other. Yasmine told him that she waited for Monica to be out of the picture so they could live their happily ever after. She was mad that he'd been ignoring her because of me. He basically told her to scram or she'd regret it. By the tone of his voice, I could tell he meant business. To be honest, it scared me. When he came back in the house, I pretended like I was oblivious. He lied and said it was his neighbor at the door. It was a lot to take in."

The internal heat turned Mark's face red. For Yasmine to say what she said about Monica made him want to turn the restaurant upside down. Kyndall patted his knee.

"I'm sorry," she expressed. "But I thought you should know."

"It's not your fault. It's the audacity of those two for me. I've known about Yasmine and Teddy. Monica knew too. She confronted him a few times, but he'd always deny it and try to make her seem like she was imagining things. The stories my sister told me are reasons why I never liked or trusted Teddy."

"I can't believe that! Teddy's always seemed so nice," Leila responded. "But I never did take to Yasmine. At the ball games, she always came off as desperate; always flirting with the team dads. She had the nerve to bat her eyelashes at Eric at the birthday party, but she quickly found out that wasn't gonna work out in her favor."

"I just feel like the whole Teddy situation is about to implode. There's too much going on. I feel it in my bones," Mark let them know. "But I don't want to put a damper on this good time. Thanks for telling me." He smiled at Kyndall despite the inner turmoil that was brewing.

She returned the smile, and they all changed the subject. After dinner, they walked outside with full bellies and leftover to-go containers. Mark checked his text message from his mother, informed them that he was going to the arcade to say "hi" to his nephew, and explained the circumstances behind the meetup.

"O wow. I'm sorry you have to go through those lengths to spend time with him." Kyndall empathized.

"It's crazy, isn't it? If I were a father, I would never take my kid through anything like that."

Kyndall was really starting to question Teddy's character the more she heard.

"So, I'll call you in the morning?" she asked before he walked away.

"Yes. It's a date," he chuckled.

"Yes, a date, but also a mission. Two birds with one stone."

They gave each other a hug and let it linger a tad bit longer than just a friendly hug.

"See you tomorrow," he whispered in her ear.

After he walked away, Leila couldn't wait to tease her sister some more. "Excuse me...cough cough...wasn't it you who was just gushing over Teddy? Now, you're gushing over Mark...really?"

Kyndall shooed her sister away. "Eric, take your wife home." She walked towards her car feeling happy and upbeat, then shouted back at them. "Love you two."

Before she made it to her car, her phone rang. It was Devon. Kyndall shook her head.

"I've got something for your ass. You just wait," she said, ignoring the call.

***

Mark slipped inside the noisy arcade that was bustling with hyper kids and exhausted parents. Cynthia, Felisha and Lil Teddy were sitting in a corner booth eating pizza, laughing and talking. Lil Teddy must have racked up on the games, because a tableful of goodies graced the table. He didn't want to interrupt his mom's precious time with Lil Teddy; he knew how much it meant to her. He was grateful to Felisha for making it happen. Instead of jeopardizing Cynthia's and Felisha's newfound understanding, he decided not to crash their little gathering.

The smiles on their faces were satisfaction enough. He'd get details from his mother later.

He was able to catch Cynthia's attention from a distance and gave her the thumbs up. She returned the gesture with a head nod. That was sufficient. He missed spending time with his nephew, but he promised himself that he'll have those days in due time. "In due time," he mumbled to himself as he exited the arcade.

Saturday Surprise!

CHAPTER SEVENTEEN
SATURDAY SURPRISE!

Every once in a while, when his son was gone, and he was feeling benevolent, Teddy would march Monica out of her prison and allow her the luxury of taking a soothing, warm bath. He figured that's the least he could do. That time had presented itself, so he ran some hot water and dropped a couple of lavender beads into the large garden bathtub. To set the mood, he turned the speaker on in the bathroom, and from his phone, streamed Monica's favorite R&B tunes. *El Debarge's* soft voice flowed through the ensuite.

He went to retrieve Monica from her cubby hole and guided her into the bathroom. She had grown accustomed to the routine. She used to beg and plead for him to release her, or she would look around to find something to whack him over the head with, but all her efforts proved fruitless. She was physically no match for Teddy. The very man who vowed to love and protect her was the very man who abused and hated her. Opening her eyes everyday had become a struggle. She was mentally and physically worn down. Teddy had gotten his wish and had broken her. She couldn't fathom living much longer and allowing him to continue to torture her. After seeing that Lil Teddy was happy and thriving without her, she'd made the decision to end it all. She no longer cared to be Teddy's slave just to be a fly on the wall in her son's life. It was unbearable.

She stood in front of the tub while Teddy watched her slip out of the unflattering muumuu, revealing her naked, frail body. She stepped robotically into the bathtub, and although the warm water was welcoming and soothing, she was in no frame of mind to appreciate or enjoy it. Once she sat in the tub, she stared off into the distance in a catatonic state and unaware of anything around except the dark cloud of Teddy standing over her like a drill sergeant.

"Enjoy it while you can. It'll be a while before you get the next one."

The bathroom's music was interrupted by his ringing phone. He ignored it the caller called again. Thinking it may be his mother, he went to pick it up from his bed, then wished he hadn't.

"Yasmine, what?!"

"Is that anyway to greet someone who you once professed your love to?"

"Yasmine, I don't have time right now."

"You never have time for me anymore, and we both know why."

"If that's why you called, then you're wasting your time."

"No...you're wasting your time. While you're entertaining your new girlfriend, seems like she's entertaining someone else."

"Jealousy is not your strong suit, Yas."

"Annnnnd...I happen to know that neither she *nor* Lil Teddy are home. Why don't you let me come by and we can have a lil chat... amongst other things?"

"What are you doing? Keeping tabs on who's in and out of my house? And as I said before, now is not the time."

"Oh, you're going to make time, Teddy!"

Meanwhile, Monica had already made up her mind. Teddy's distraction was just what she needed. The day she saw the woman who was reading with Lil Teddy, that was all the confirmation she needed in order to follow through with her plan to end her suffering. She closed her eyes and slid beneath the surface of the water. All she wanted was enough time to accomplish her goal before Teddy returned. She'd already mustered up the courage to go through with it since she figured she was already in hell; anyplace else would be welcome. She held her breath at first, then released, allowing the water to fill her insides and infiltrate her lungs until her mind went completely blank and her body felt weightless. What remained of her soul, left her eyes and her thin hair swayed with the flow of the water.

Highly annoyed with Yasmine, Teddy yelled into the speaker of the phone. "Goodbye, Yas! I told you I'm busy and that's that!"

"Teddy, don't you dare!"

The line went dead.

Teddy went back inside the ensuite only to see Monica's seemingly lifeless body in the tub with her bulged eyes staring up at him. With the speed of lightning, he raced to lift her out of the tub and laid her limp body on the floor to perform CPR.

With each chest press, he shouted, "Wake up! I get to decide when you die, not you! Wake up!"

From the way that Teddy had been recently acting, Yasmine expected him not to give in to her advances, so she already had a trick up her sleeve. As an active volunteer parent at the school, she was able to swindle Lil Teddy's house key from his bookbag. She had firsthand knowledge that he kept the extra key in his backpack in case of emergencies. Never thinking that she'd ever have to stoop so low, Yasmine felt that she was out of options; Teddy left her no choice.

She was already parked outside his house when she called and was hoping since he was home alone that he'd invite her inside. *So much for assuming and wishing.* She took the key out of her purse. "That's fine, though, Teddy. I'm inviting myself, and once you see me, I'm sure you'll find me hard to resist. Besides, what I have to show you, I know you'll thank me later." She looked at the pictures she'd taken earlier.

Forgoing knocking on the door, she slid the key in the lock and let herself in as if she belonged there. Once inside, she closed it without making a sound, and put her phone and purse on the sofa. She needed her hands free so she could slip out of her clothes and give Teddy a nice surprise. From the living room to the kitchen, she made a trail of garments and left her panties at the entrance to the bedroom door.

After creeping inside the bedroom, she heard music coming from the bathroom and smelled the faint traces of lavender.

"O...bath time," she giddily mumbled. Like a cat on the prowl, she tiptoed her naked body in the bathroom, and what she saw made her scream out in confusion and horror.

"Monica!? Oh my God! Noooo....Teddy...noooo!"

Simultaneously, Monica's body shook as she violently coughed up the water she'd ingested while Teddy sat on his knees pressing on her chest. Yasmine's sudden appearance startled him, and he looked up with eyes the size of saucers having been caught in the act. She took in Monica's frail body lying on the floor. She was a shell of her former self, but it was undoubtedly Monica.

Yasmine covered her open mouth with her hands. Teddy saw the mortification in her eyes.

"O my goodness, Teddy!" she finally said.

They were both paralyzed for a spell, each not knowing how to react to their own respective shock, while Monica lay in distress, coughing and heaving in oxygen. Yasmine's flight instincts kicked in, and she no longer craved Teddy's attention. The puzzle pieces floating in her head started to take shape and the bigger picture slowly became evident. She immediately felt exposed. Any ideas of seducing and confronting Teddy quickly went out the window. She ran out of the room, causing Teddy to panic. He forgot all about Monica, jumped up and ran towards Yasmine. Before she could get too far, he grabbed her from behind, while she violently kicked and screamed.

"Why couldn't you just have stayed away like I told you too?"

"Teddy! Put me down! I'm sorry."

Her request fell on deaf ears. She had seen too much, and he was faced with a dilemma. He threw her naked body on the bed. Frightened, she tried to scurry away from him. This Teddy was someone new; she was not familiar with this Teddy. She feared for her life. The vision of

Monica laid out on the bathroom floor was imprinted on her brain. The questions that swirled in her mind regarding Monica's disappearance were plentiful. She was confused, but at the moment, concerned about getting out of there alive. *Who is this man?!*

She tried to kick him, then picked up a book that was on the bed and threw it at him. He ducked, then proceeded to put his fingers around her throat to subdue her. Her eyes rounded as she tried with all her might to pry his fingers from around her neck. She kicked and flailed relentlessly until the wind left her body, and she went limp on the bed.

Teddy's chest heaved up and down as he stood in a demonic trance over Yasmine's body that was sprawled across his disheveled bed. Monica's persistent cough broke him from his stupor, causing him to rush back into the bathroom to quickly figure out his next move.

An hour later

Yasmine slowly opened her eyes, continually opening and closing them due to the harsh light. She placed her hand on her banging head. The headache was pounding away inside her skull. Within minutes, she finally lifted her head away from the corner of the wall that she was sitting against and noticed the oversized white t-shirt that covered her body. Confusion clouded her thoughts. She felt her throat and recalled Teddy choking her out. *Where am I?*

The stainless steel sink and the toilet in the corner looked like a jail cell. She saw the tv monitor in the top corner of the small room. The monitor showed herself and another person. Her eyes rounded as the realization of what happened came to her. Her head snapped to the right and saw Monica laid out on the small bed with her eyes barely open looking sick and discolored.

"Oh My God!" She cried out. "Oh My God! Oh My God!"

Panic started to take over. She jumped up and took off towards the opening and tried to pry it open. It was sealed shut. Her eyes scanned the entire layout of the small space and didn't see one thing that she could use to help pry the door open. Then she thought about her phone that she left in the living room along with her clothes when she unlawfully entered Teddy's home in her twisted attempt to confront him and win back his affections.

"Teddy!" she screamed. "Teddy! Let me out! I promise I won't tell! Let me ouuuut!"

She looked at Monica again and couldn't believe that the woman was alive, although barely, and right up under everyone's noses. And to know that Teddy had her tucked away inside their house made her insides churn.

"I'm gonna be sick." She bent over clutching her stomach and wishing the sensation would subside.

After a minute of letting the wave of nausea fade, she realized the dire situation she had gotten herself in. She slid down the side of the door with her knees pressed against her chest and cried.

Teddy stood in his bedroom and watched the monitor and saw that Yasmine had come to and was in the middle of having a meltdown. He was at a loss of what to do next. She just had to show up and throw a monkey wrench in his system. *How did she even get in ? Why couldn't she just listen?* He paced the length of his bedroom, irate and mumbling to himself. He felt like banging his head against the wall. Monica's suicide attempt and Yasmine's pop-up couldn't have happened at a more inopportune time.

"Uhhhhhgggg!" he shouted.

The only silver lining is that Lil Teddy is with my mom this weekend, he thought. *That gives me just a little time to figure this out.*

When he walked outside his bedroom, he saw Yasmine's panties on the floor. He shook his head and picked them up, then followed the trail to his living room where a few of her belongings were. The buzzing phone took him by surprise. He looked down at the screen. It was Yasmine's mother, Miss Ruby, calling.

"Shit! Shit! Shit!" He punched the inside of his hand. "Think, Teddy, think." He hurriedly picked up all of Yasmine's things and threw them on a pile on the couch.

Yasmine's phone buzzed again with a text message. He glared at the message.

Why aren't you answering your phone? I thought you'd be back by now

Teddy pondered a response.

I'll be home tomorrow. I decided to take a long drive and get a room tonight to clear my mind

He waited for the reply

You have a son to take care of. I know you're not in your feelings about that no good man

Teddy sucked his teeth at the audacity. He didn't care for Miss Ruby either. The apple definitely didn't fall too far from the tree, and after years of dealing with Yasmine, he realized why both women were single and miserable.

Bye mom. Kiss Antonio for me. ttyl

Frustrated, he threw the phone on the couch. He could imagine the prune-face expression that Miss Ruby was probably giving at that moment. Yasmine had definitely put a kink in his routine. He was faced with the task of trying to figure out how he was going to deal with her. It was going to take some finagling, but he had to work quickly, especially after he looked out the window and saw her car parked outside. Shaking his head, he knew he had to get rid of it and fast. A couple of young goons who wouldn't mind taking it for a "joy" ride came to mind, but before he could make that call, Yasmine's phone buzzed again. He picked it up and checked the message.

Can I see you tonight beautiful

Teddy's eyebrows shot up. It never occurred to him that Yasmine was seeing someone else. He thought she was loyal to him in spite of him giving her the cold shoulder. He looked at the sender. Seth.

"The coach? Damn."

Deciding to humor Coach Seth, Teddy responded.

I can't tonight. I made plans already

What do I need to do to get you to change your mind?

Before Teddy could respond, a picture of Seth's unflattering private part popped up. Teddy instantly became infuriated. Without thinking, he marched towards his bedroom, grabbed his remote and entered the hideaway.

"I knew you were a simple slut when I met you!" His voice boomed through the tiny space, startling Yasmine from her quiet cries.

He grabbed her up by the t-shirt and pointed the phone in her face. "This! Is this what you like?!"

"Teddy! Stop! Noooo...let me out of here," she cried. "I promise I won't tell. Please!"

"You been fucking the coach too?!"

She peered at the phone through red, tearful eyes. "No, Teddy. I promise."

"So, he's just texting you a picture of his dick for no reason, huh?" He held the phone closer to her face.

Sobbing, "We went on one date. That's it. You were ignoring me."

"I don't believe you!"

In the midst of Teddy and Yasmine's lovers quarrel, Monica was still in a fragile state. Her weakened body and mind could care less what they were arguing about. She just wanted to drift off to sleep and never wake up. Her listless body and her rolling eyes were an indication that she was floating between two worlds—the known and the unknown.

"If you don't trust me, look at the text thread," she tried to reason.

He loosened his grip on the t-shirt and scrolled through the text messages while Yasmine groveled at his feet. He opened up her photo gallery to verify the truth but didn't make it past the last few pictures that Yasmine had captured of Felisha, Lil Teddy and Cynthia, which made his temper rise. But when he saw the picture of Kyndall with Mark, he lost it.

"What the fuck!"

18

Ambush

C HAPTER EIGHTEEN
AMBUSH

Sunday morning, Mark sat on the recliner across from his mother and couldn't help but smile at her as she happily expressed how she felt about her outing with Lil Teddy and Felisha.

"I'm just happy that Felisha agreed to let me see him," Cynthia explained to him. "We actually have a little bit in common. Can you believe that?" she laughed.

Mark wasn't overjoyed at the thought of Felisha *or* her son, but he did appreciate the effort she put forth in letting Cynthia see her grandson.

"No, I can't believe it. You two are nothing alike, but as long as you two can co-exist and share in your love for Lil Teddy, I guess I can't be too hard on her."

"She's actually going to bring him by today. I'm going to bake him some chocolate chip cookies!" Cynthia was elated.

"I would stick around, but I have something to do." His phone buzzed. "And that's my something right there." He read the text message:

All set!

"That's my cue. Make sure to tell my nephew I love him and to text me from his phone. Just don't tell him that around Felisha. I still don't trust her."

"Son, you don't trust anybody," she giggled as she got up from the couch and headed to the kitchen to begin baking the chocolate chip cookies.

Thirty minutes later, Mark sat in the corner of the café seeming to be just an ordinary customer enjoying his morning coffee and pastry. No one was the wiser that he was there as a watchdog to make sure that Kyndall's plan to ambush Devon didn't go awry.

Mark sat back in the chair in his own thoughts, looking over at Kyndall who sat at a table near the entrance waiting for Devon to arrive. *What type of man takes a wonderful woman through all of this? A freaking clown...typical narcissist who thinks he can get any woman he wants, put them under his "spell" and treat them like trash once he gets them where he wants them.* He bit into his flaky glazed croissant. *If I were lucky enough to get a prize like Kyndall, I'd treat her like the precious jewel that she is. She can't be fully aware of her worth by dealing with clowns like Devon AND Ted.* Mark sucked his teeth at the thought of Ted.

He watched the way Devon smirked at Kyndall when he walked into the café. That self-assured smirk that he felt could get him anything and anybody he wanted. Devon looked like the typical black fraternity brother—physically fit, clean cut, nicely dressed, boy-next-door good looks—a wolf in sheep's clothing. Mark silently chuckled at the man's "confidence".

Devon sat down at the table with Kyndall and immediately started his spiel. "I was pleasantly surprised that you finally agreed to meet with me. You know I've been trying my hardest to show you how much I miss you and how much you mean to me. This is definitely a step in the right direction." When he reached out to touch her hand, she pulled back.

"Baby, you don't have to keep pushing back. I just want to show you from now on how much I've changed. You can feel safe with me. I need you back in my life." He laid it on thick.

Kyndall nodded, pretending to be interested in what he was saying while thinking what a loser he really was. Little did he know that her phone was underneath the napkin and the caller could hear their conversation. She wanted him to sink himself further.

"Devon, it's hard for me to sit across from you and take everything you say for face value. You've hurt me more than once, and I forgave you more than once. How many more times do you expect me to go down this road with you?"

They were momentarily interrupted by the waitress who took their orders and vanished. After the waitress left, Kyndall saw the wheels turning in his head contemplating how he was going to finesse her with his next set of words. He carefully crafted what he planned to say as he stared deeply into her eyes with "sincerity" and "love".

"Kyndall, I realized these past few weeks that I truly messed up. It hurts me to know that I hurt you. You're the love of my life. You're the future mother of my child. I can't live without you."

She thought she saw him conjure up a way to make his eyes wet. She couldn't believe she had once fallen in love with this man and was so blinded that she couldn't see the snake that he really was. She couldn't stomach anymore of his affirmations of love. Instead of responding to him, she picked up her phone and spoke to the person who was hanging on to everything that was being said.

"You can take it from here. I've heard enough," Kyndall told the person on the other end of the line.

The puzzled look on Devon's face turned to pure shock when his pregnant fiancé, Vanessa, rushed through the door in a fit of rage, not caring about causing a scene.

"Soooo, she's the love of your life, huh?! The future mother of your child, huh!?" she yelled, rubbing her protruding belly.

Vanessa flung her purse and clocked Devon in his head.

"Vanessa!" he shouted.

"Don't Vanessa me! You lying, dirty dick snake! I'm carrying your child and you act like I don't exist! I swear I'm gonna make you regret the day you ever told the first lie! Pathetic loser!"

Kyndall shook her head at Devon before she got up to walk away from the table. There was nothing else for her to say. He was Vanessa's problem and no longer hers. She had dodged a bullet. She would hate to have to be in Vanessa's shoes. She joined Mark at his table, and they both started laughing uncontrollably like two best friends privy to a secret joke. They watched Devon try to get up from his seat all while trying to shield himself from Vanessa's wild and explosive blows. The waitress tried to verbally intervene, but a few members of the staff from the back came out to try to carefully restrain the irate pregnant woman. Mark and Kyndall continued to laugh at Devon who was finally able to jump away from the table and run out the door with a pregnant track star hot on his heels.

"Damn! Did you see how far his eyes came outta his head when she popped up at the table?" Mark couldn't stop laughing.

"Yes! He looked like a completely different person. All I've got left to say is good riddance!"

Once Mark wiped the tears from his eyes and they both had time to quiet down, he looked at her with genuine concern. "Are you okay?"

"Yes, thanks for asking. I knew I was already done with him, but now HE knows. I want to thank you for coming here with me as my bodyguard," she smirked. "I think I can get used to your services."

"You're welcome," he blushed. "Honestly, though, I wouldn't have wanted you to deal with that all by yourself, just in case he wanted to fly off the handle. And speaking of bodyguard...I'm more than happy to be on your team. Can I get a t-shirt made?"

"You've earned it. By all means."

"I like the sound of that. What do you have planned for the rest of the day," he asked.

"My calendar is open."

"So is mine. Why don't we go find something fun to do and enjoy the rest of this day?"

They high fived and hightailed it out of the café on to their next adventure.

***

Teddy had a busy morning trying to tie up a few loose ends. First, he made his way to the unsavory part of town and recruited two goons to "repossess" Yasmine's car from his street and paid them handsomely to "make it disappear." They gladly accepted the challenge and promised him that snitching was against their code, so he didn't have to worry about them once the deed was done. He gave them the car keys and Yasmine's phone and told them where they could find the car.

Next, he set out to see his mother. After seeing the pictures in Yasmine's phone, Teddy needed answers from Felisha as to why she would go against his wishes and betray him by meeting up with Cynthia. She wasn't at home, so he rode by Cynthia's house, and sure enough, he caught Felisha and Lil Teddy walking into the home of his estranged mother-in-law. He couldn't control the steam coming out of his ears as his blood pressure began to rise. Felisha was the only person he felt he could ever fully trust. Anger and hurt set in. His mother knew his disdain for his in-laws and their holier than thou attitudes, thinking they were above everyone else. They never saw him casually stroll by, but he certainly planned to confront Felisha at the first chance he got.

On top of Felisha's disloyalty, he couldn't for the life of him figure out why Kyndall and crew were hanging out with Mark. *When did that happen?* He repeatedly asked himself throughout his fitful night. Has she been in cahoots with Mark this whole time? He thought he and Kyndall had something special, and she was with him when Mark attacked him. *Is that why? Did I misread the signs?* So many unanswered questions invaded his mind. As he drove, his vision began to blur with rage. The thought of Kyndall and Mark together made him even more furious and vengeful. Like an old, dilapidated dam, he felt like he was ready to burst at any given moment. He had some thinking to do and some plans to execute. "Nobody is going to be laughing behind my back when it's all said and done. NOBODY!"

***

The despair that Yasmine felt was like none other. Never had she experienced the level of helplessness that she was currently experiencing. To ever think that Teddy was a monster never crossed her mind. She had been so blinded by her infatuation disguised as love for him that she misread all the red flags. As she looked over at Moncia, who looked like she was part ghost and part human, she was frightened at what was to become of her. If Teddy could lock up his wife for two years and let the world believe that she had vanished, and even keep her away from their son, there would be no telling what he would do to her.

The realization of how dire her situation was, had Yasmine on the verge of depression and desperation. Facing the unknown, she wanted to cleanse her spirit and start by apologizing to Monica. Compassion and humanity took a front seat to competitiveness, envy and greed. None of the latter things mattered anymore. Looking back on her disrespectful behavior towards Monica, made her sick. *Why did it take this extreme turn of events for me to see the error of my ways? Would Teddy keep me locked up just as long? Would my mother send the cops over here to look for me? What would Antonio do without me?* The questions flooded her brain.

"Oh my God! I gotta get outta here!" she screamed, causing Monica to open her eyes even more.

"This is what you wanted," Monica finally spoke in a slow, barely audible, monotonous tone. "Welcome to my world."

Yasmine held her hand over her mouth as the tears rained down her face.

19

Sunday Funday

C HAPTER NINETEEN
SUNDAY FUNDAY

What started out as an ambush to confront Devon about the double life he was living, turned into a laugh fest between Mark and Kyndall who were doubled over in laughter reliving the earlier event.

"I'm not laughing at his girlfriend's pain, but that was too funny not to crack up. That was the best comedy show I'd been to in forever." Mark wiped the wetness from the corner of his eye.

"And he deserved every fist that landed on him...plus some," Kyndall agreed.

Once they left the café after encountering Devon, Kyndall dropped her car off at home, got in the car with Mark, and they went to a popular brunch spot, where they were currently on their umpteenth unlimited mimosa. The table was littered with remnants of waffles, chicken, syrup, hot sauce, hashbrowns and eggs.

"Plus some is right," he chuckled, then took inventory of all the food they had eaten and at his remaining glass of mimosa. "You know what? This is my first brunch experience. I'm actually having a fun time."

"Are you kidding me?"

"No. My mother and sister used to try to drag me with them, but I always thought it was a girly thing. Is this what I've been missing?"

"Yes! Who doesn't like good food and unlimited sugary drinks?" she asked, downing the last bit of her drink.

"Just don't tell your brother-in-law. I have a workout session with him tomorrow?"

She put her finger to her lips. "Mums the word."

"So, what's next on your day's itinerary?" he asked.

"Not much."

"Would you like to take a ride with me? I think I like this hanging-out-with-you thing."

"Really?" she grinned. "It *has* been fun. Why not? Where are we going?"

"Nowhere far. You'll like it. I promise."

"Are you good enough to drive?"

He nodded. "Trust me. Besides, I wouldn't let anything happen to the precious cargo."

Kyndall smiled brightly, turned on by his flirty comeback. "In that case..."

After settling comfortably in the passenger seat of Mark's BMW, Kyndall checked her phone and saw that her sister had called a couple times. She didn't want to interrupt the flow of the afternoon, but it could have been important, so she decided to call back. Immediately upon answering the phone, Leila got straight to the point.

"Sis, where are you?"

"I'm out. What's going on?"

"We had a visitor come by the house," Leila informed. "Yasmine's mother. The one you were talking about who showed up at Teddy's house."

Mark looked over at the puzzlement etched on Kyndall's face "Anything wrong?" he whispered after turning the music down.

She shrugged.

"What would her mother come to *your* house for?"

"She said that her daughter is not answering her phone; it's going to voicemail, and the last text she got said that she was going to a hotel."

"That doesn't sound unusual. Maybe she needed a break, but still, why would her mom come to your house?"

"She said she went by Teddy's, but he wasn't there, so she decided to reach out to all the other team parents."

The reality of what Leila was implying slowly started to sink in. Her quietness confirmed what Leila thought it would.

"You don't think she thinks that something fishy happened?" Kyndall questioned and put the phone on speaker to let Mark know what they were talking about.

"All I know is...if the lady was concerned enough to be knocking on people's doors, she may have a reason to be concerned, but I really don't know what to think. She mentioned that Yasmine has never been unreachable and not be in constant contact with her son. She guessed from Yasmine's last text that she went by Teddy's and the conversation didn't go over too well."

At the mention of Teddy's name, Mark's eyebrows furrowed and his ears perked up.

"Hmmm...." Kyndall said. "Maybe she's overreacting."

"Could be...but the only thing that makes me question it is the fact that you said you heard Yasmine and Teddy arguing."

Taking a deep breath, Kyndall tried not to let her mind wander. "You know I like Teddy. This is just too close for comfort."

Mark inwardly groaned at Kyndall's praise of Teddy.

"Hopefully, it's just a case of her mother being overprotective and worried and nothing more. Maybe Yasmine did just need a break and went off the grid for a minute." Leila tried to reason. "I just can't get that worried look out of my head. I felt so bad for her. She also said if Yasmine doesn't materialize by the end of the day, she's filing a missing person's report."

Mark's heart fell. Hearing that took him back to the time he and his family did the exact same thing...file a missing person's report. But what good did that do? He shook his head. He wouldn't wish that feeling on anybody...to have a missing loved one and not know if they were dead or alive or out there somewhere in pain. The thought just made him ill.

He didn't care for Yasmine, but the humanity in him took a front seat to his disdain for her.

"Oh wow," was all Kyndall could muster up. She knew it was perhaps a sore subject for Mark.

"I just wanted to make sure you were good," Leila told her. "I don't want to put out a missing person's report on you."

"I'm good, sis. Thanks for letting me know. I'll call you later."

"Okay. Love you."

She disconnected the line and looked over at Mark who seemed to be deep in thought as he continued to drive to their destination.

"Are you sure you still want to stay on this journey? That was a lot."

"I'm not gonna let their drama come in between our Sunday Funday," he smiled. "I can worry about that tomorrow, but right now, let's enjoy the moment."

That infectious and bright smile that he found to be one of her best traits was her response, and all the negative energy from Leila's phone call was automatically tossed out the window.

"In that case, Sunday Funday is in full effect!" Kyndall connected her playlist to the speaker and turned the music volume up. The Ying Yang Twins' *Salt Shaker* blasted through the speakers, and she started to bounce in her seat.

Mark was not used to letting his hair down, but he let go of his uptight and conservative disposition to match Kyndall's vivacious energy, and it felt good. They forgot all the problems of the world and rode in crunk-music bliss until they got off the interstate and rode along the coast.

"The beach?" she rhetorically stated while catching glimpses of the ocean in between the high-rise oceanside buildings.

It was early evening and the sun had simmered down just a bit. They both let the windows down to take advantage of the natural ocean breeze air conditioner.

"The water has a calming effect. I love it here. I hope you don't mind me driving us here."

"Of course not. It's the perfect day for it." Kyndall was amped.

He drove a few more miles to a sea-colored high-rise, pressed a gate code into the garage, and parked in a designated reserved spot.

"I take it this is your hideaway that you mentioned before?"

With immense pride, Mark said, "Yes. I want to show it off to you. Aside from that, it's been a minute since I've checked on the place."

Holding her hand to her heart, she replied, "I feel special."

He quickly got out and opened the door for her, grabbing her hand to help her out.

"As you should. You're my first guest in over two years."

"Wow. Now I really feel special."

He led the way to the elevator, and they got off at the fifth floor. When he unlocked the door to his condo and guided her inside, she was instantly impressed with the simplicity and the beauty of the silver and teal décor and the shiny, white floor. She was instantly drawn to the balcony that served as a centerpiece to the massive, blue ocean out in the distance.

"This is heaven," she said, walking in a trance to the French doors that stood in the way of her and paradise. "May I?" she asked before opening the doors.

"Be my guest."

He stood behind and watched her lean against the rail of the balcony, taking in the scenery beyond and below—the sparkling pool, the tiki hut, the ocean, the seagulls, his own private resort whenever he needed a break from the mundane and the hectic pressures of life. He hadn't entertained any guests since before Monica's disappearance. His mind wouldn't let him focus on anything other than his immediate family matters. Kyndall brought out a side to him that had been dormant for far too long. She made him want to enjoy the everyday pleasures that life had to offer. The way he was drawn to her caught him pleasingly off guard, and he didn't want to waste anymore life by not living. The time had come for him to no longer play it safe and to take the bull by the horns. *Fuck Big Ted!* he thought.

He turned on the music, changing the mood to a relaxed, R&B vibe. Maxwell's *Ascension* drifted through the condo.

"Would you like some wine, liquor or water?" he asked, breaking her trance.

She turned around to look at him. "You think we still got room for more adult beverages in our system?"

"Need I remind you...it's Sunday Funday. It's whatever. And if you need to sleep it off, I have an extra room."

"Oooo...I see I just created a monster," she laughed. "How can a girl say no to that then? I'll have some red wine. Cabernet if you will."

When Mark joined her on the balcony with two glasses of red wine, she had already taken a seat on one of the chairs separated by a small table. He proposed they do a toast and she happily agreed.

"To Sunday Funday with a beautiful lady."

"To Sunday Funday with a handsome, considerate man."

They clinked their glasses, took a sip and sat back, enjoying the sounds of the ocean. Mark was grateful that Kyndall trusted him enough to make the drive with him. He was thoroughly enjoying her company and didn't want to part ways so soon. Not knowing if and when the opportunity would present itself again, he took the initiative to continue their outing.

"Thanks for blessing my home with your presence."

"Thanks for inviting me. This is beautiful."

"I didn't get to give you the tour, though. You came straight out here," he chuckled.

She palmed her face. "Oh my goodness! I know. I'm sorry. The view was calling me, and the more I look down at that pool, I wanna jump in. Why did you bring me to the water, and I'm not dressed to get wet?"

He grinned and let that sexual innuendo hang in the air before he responded.

"If you really wanna get wet, then my sister had some bathing suits in the spare room that she never even took the tags off. When she and Lil Teddy came over for family beach days, they would use the other room.

You and she are about the same size if you wanna take a look at what's in there."

Knowing how delicate the situation was with his sister, she felt that she didn't want to impose. Mark caught a sense of her feelings and let her know that it was okay.

"Really. I insist," he told her. "I haven't been as sensitive as I've been in the past. I've been feeling okay, so come on. Let's take a look."

He put their wine glasses on the table, helped her up from the chair and led her into the second bedroom.

"This is Monica and Lil Teddy's designated space when they visit."

"Ahh. This is so nice." She admired the canvas photos on the walls—the sunset, the water washing ashore the beach, and the one of Lil Teddy and his mom posing in the beach sand. The queen-size bed with the light blue comforter was the focal point of the room with the addition of seashell lamps and a decorative surfboard in the corner that gave it a beachy aesthetic.

Mark went into the closet and pulled out a few bathing suits that still had tags on them.

"See...my sister still has brand new things in this closet. The bathroom's right there. Help yourself. There's everything in there that you could possibly need. I'll be on the balcony waiting."

Kyndall walked into the bathroom and couldn't help but be enamored by Mark's generosity. Maybe there was a whole lot of truth to what Eric said...Mark is a good man.

"He gets my stamp of approval, too." Kyndall said to herself in the mirror, repeating the words that Eric had stated about Mark.

Not-So-Fun Sunday

CHAPTER TWENTY
NOT-SO-FUN SUNDAY

Teddy's day was met with one disappointment after another. Having to deal with Yasmine finding out about Monica had really thrown a curveball into his mix. His mind was racing trying to figure out his next move. He was not going to be able to dodge another round of questioning if another woman was reported missing on his watch. Not only was he stressed out about Yasmine's infiltration into his life, but finding out that his mother betrayed him by secretly meeting with Cynthia made him feel like she had dug a dagger in his back. After all they had endured together, to him, his mother was the one and only woman whom he thought he could count on no matter what. He thought she would at least show undying gratitude for the lengths he went through by releasing them both from his father's tyranny even though she was in the dark about his direct involvement.

To add insult to injury, Kyndall was not answering any of her calls or texts. Just to know that she and Mark were cozied up with one another shot his blood pressure through the roof. Every woman in his life had caused him enough pain, anger, embarrassment and aggravation. He was ready to unleash. As he sat in front of her house, he tried Kyndall's number again. Still no answer. Her car was there, so she must be home, he surmised. He was compelled to get down to the nitty gritty of her and Mark's "friendship."

After so long, all sense and caring went out the window. He got out his truck and rang her doorbell. Then he knocked loudly beginning to act like a stalkerish lover. Kyndall's neighbor peeked out the door, and after giving Teddy the once over, let him know, "She's not there. Can I tell her who came by looking?"

Teddy glazed over at the woman with the dark complexion, cat eyes and banging body dressed in short shorts with fat thighs and a bra top with ample cleavage hanging out. By the way she was eyeing him, he picked up on the flirtatious vibes.

"I was worried. She hasn't answered her phone, but her car is here."

"Oh, that's because she got in the car with a nice looking man and they rode off in a black beamer with a UCF tag on the back. He opened the car door for her and everything," she explained. "She must really be on her hot girl, cause you are like the third man I've seen come around her for my girl, Kyndall. I don't know what I'm doing wrong, but I need to sit her down and ask for some pointers."

Although Kyndall's neighbor was gorgeous in her own right, Teddy paid no attention to her or her rambling. All he heard was 'black beamer' and he knew without a doubt it was Mark. He thanked her for the information and walked back to his truck in a pissed daze.

"If Kyndall don't work out for you, I'll be around!" she shouted out before he got into his truck.

His light complexion turned red, the tips of his ears and his nose were flushed. To know that Mark and Kyndall had run off somewhere, and she was ignoring his calls, took him to a darker place. All care and rationality had ceased. He felt betrayed on all ends of the spectrum. It was time to take drastic measures and execute a new plan.

***

"Monica, you have to eat something."

Yasmine held up the Swiss turkey sandwich that Teddy so kindly left behind, along with two bottles of water. She'd been trying to coax Monica to at least take a small bite; she looked like she was withering away, and Yasmine didn't want that additional problem on her hands. Since they'd been confined together, Yasmine could tell that her roommate was getting weaker. She looked frail and sickly. The two women were never friends—each on opposite sides of Teddy vying for his love and attention; Monica rightly so, since she *was* his wife. Yasmine never considered the woman's feelings once Teddy showed interest. All she cared about was pushing his wife to the side and taking her place as the only woman on his arms and in his bed.

As she stared at the helpless woman, she felt terrible, realizing what the woman must have endured at the hands of Teddy a/k/a Jekyll & Hyde. He had everyone fooled except Monica. It was apparent that Monica no longer cared about living. She was starving herself. Yasmine's efforts to get her to eat were futile. She put the sandwich down, kneeled down on the floor near the edge of the bed, and looked into the eyes of her "rival."

"Monica...I'm soooo sorry. I know that probably sounds foolish each time I say it, but I don't know any other way to express that. I haven't always made the best choices in men, and when Teddy came along, he seemed like the real deal, the perfect gentleman. I knew he was married, but he said he was unhappy and was leaving you. That's no excuse. I was selfish, foolish, dumb, blinded, and so many other things. I promise if we make it out of here, I will get help. I will work on myself and will make it up to you however I can. I know it feels useless for me to say all this right now, but Monica, I need you to want to live. We have sons out there who need their mamas. Please, Monica, eat. We need to put our heads together and get out of here! Please, Monica, please!" She cried an endless stream of tears and shook the lady, hoping her words and her apology registered.

Staring into Monica's soulless eyes, Yasmine felt it was her duty to try her damndest to get them out of Teddy's prison. But how?

***

Leila decided to take her sister's advice to stop being paranoid and overly emotional. With all the glorious years that she and Eric shared, she knew that her husband adored and cherished her. There had to be a good explanation behind the subtle changes, the phone calls, and the lipstick on his shirt. She'd just have to ask him about it. They were always honest and upfront with each other, so why should this time be any different. That sit down would have to wait, though. They both had been so busy that they hadn't had time for intimacy, so Leila took it upon herself to plan a date night. Since Julian didn't have school on Monday, due to a student holiday and teacher workday *(since when did the schools start doing that?)*, she took him to his uncle's house to spend the night with his cousins. Eric was at the gym tying up loose ends in the office to get the week started without a hitch. That gave her the time she needed to get ready.

Dusk had set; the evening air was warm and breezy. It was the perfect evening for a picnic in the yard. Leila stepped outside into their resort-style backyard and set up the romantic ambiance inside the screened gazebo that stood in the corner of the yard. She lit candles and placed them on the table along with an ice bucket of champagne and a bowl of strawberries and pineapples. The lobster, steak and potatoes that she prepared earlier were placed in the warmer in the kitchen. After setting the mood, she took a soothing bath, moisturized her body with a strawberry scent, fluffed her hair, letting it hang free, then she put on her Beyonce-inspired black lace bodysuit and feather heels. She twirled in the mirror and smiled.

"Damn, girl, you look good," she told herself.

Eric was usually home no later than eight-o-clock, so she stepped outside and waited for him on the chaise lounger on the covered lanai while she sipped on some rum punch that she concocted earlier. She turned on some 90s R&B, chomped on a few strawberries and continued to sip, awaiting her unsuspecting husband to arrive.

A few hours later

Leila thought she was dreaming as she barely heard Eric's voice and him gently touching her shoulder to shake her awake.

"Baby, wake up." He slowly noticed the sexy attire she had on, the music, the decorated gazebo, and the empty glass of punch next to her and recognized the lengths she went through to surprise him. He closed his eyes and shook his head.

She opened her eyes and let the brain fog dissipate before she realized she fell asleep.

"What time is it?"

"10:30."

"10:30! Eric, you're late!" She jumped up from the lounger and rushed inside the house, leaving her heels outside.

He watched her sexy body bounce into the kitchen and saw her phone sitting on the table. He knew then that he had messed up. From the looks of it, she had planned a date night and didn't get his text message. He exhaled sharply, knowing he was about to get the silent treatment. She pulled the food from the warmer and threw the pan down on the stove.

"Now the food's all dry!"

"Baby, I'm sorry. I called and left you a message. Drew called right before I was leaving the gym. He was having some issues and needed a listening ear. We met at the bar, so he could vent about all his problems. I'll make it up to you," he said, moving in closer to embrace her.

"Don't touch me! You're never late! All of a sudden you need to play Dr. Phil! I'm not buying it!"

"It's not *that* late, Leila. Come on. We still have the rest of the night. Don't fly off the handle."

"Don't fly off the handle?! Are you serious...and I got all cute for nothing!" She looked down at the lace ensemble she had on.

"And you look beautiful." He hoped the compliment would melt the ice.

"Don't try to flatter me! Your dinner is served. Or did you already eat with Drew?"

She stormed out of the kitchen and into the bedroom, slamming the door behind her.

"Damn." He stood in the kitchen and sighed.

Sunday Night Blues

CHAPTER TWENTY-ONE
SUNDAY NIGHT BLUES

When Teddy finally made it back home from Kyndall's place, feelings of rage and disappointment in people he thought he could trust, ate him up. He felt a sense of betrayal, and his vindictive nature began to reignite itself. The last thing he wanted to do was deal with Yasmine's mom waiting outside his house. *Shit's about to get real*, he thought. He parked his truck inside the garage then stepped out to meet her. She had already gotten out of her car and was rushing to him before he fully emerged from the garage.

"Hi Teddy. I know it's late, and I hate to bother you, but I'm worried about Yasmine. She hasn't been in touch since yesterday, and her phone goes straight to voicemail."

He knew that Yasmine's phone could be tracked to his house, so he needed to answer the question smartly and buy some time to throw her off the scent.

"Miss Ruby, I honestly don't think there's anything to worry about. Yasmine came by to pick up a gift bag I had for Antonio, then she mentioned needing some down time. She sounded like she was going to take an excursion, but she didn't give me any details. And by the way, I hope Antonio's recovering nicely."

"Yes, he is, thanks. But, back to the subject of why I'm here, Teddy. I know about yours and Yasmine's dalliances. I've known for a long time. I don't agree with it, and I told my daughter countless times how I felt.

She's a grown woman, though, and very stubborn. There was nothing I could do or say to persuade her otherwise. Have you two had an argument or disagreement? I'm very worried. It's not usual for her to not have her phone on and check on Antonio."

"No, we did not have an argument. She may not have liked me telling her that I needed some space, but that's the gist of it. If she said she needed some time alone, then that's most likely what it is. I say give her some time to unwind," he told her. "To be honest, there are moments when I need some quiet time. I go fishing and turn off my phone just to relax. Ask my mom. She tried to contact me during one of my off-the-grid times. Yasmine will be okay. If I hear from her before you do, I'll be sure to let her know you came by."

Miss Ruby sighed. "You may be right, but I'm only giving her another day. Her non-communication is not acceptable. She's a mother for God's sake." Miss Ruby turned to walk back to her car. "I'm sorry I bothered you," she turned around to say.

Following behind, Teddy tried to reassure her before she left. "It's no problem, Miss Ruby. Go home and take care of Antonio. There's no school tomorrow, so Yasmine is probably taking advantage of that. I'll try to reach her as well."

"Thank you, Teddy. Hopefully, I'll hear from her soon."

Once she drove off, Teddy immediately felt the pressure, and time was of the essence. Yasmine had brought unnecessary drama to his home, and it was now time to execute his exit plan. He had a few duffle bags of necessary items for him and Lil Teddy that he had packed over the course of the year and tossed them in the backseat of his truck. He made sure he had money, fake I.D.s, passports, clothes and a few mementos. He felt that the day would come sooner or later that he would need to leave his life in *Calm Springs* behind. With years of Monica's incessant threats of leaving and taking his son, he had taken small steps to start a quiet, new life in a rural area far away from Florida He wistfully thought of a cabin in Maine, Alaska or Washington. He and Lil Teddy would go fishing, boating, snow skiing, woodchopping, and experience all kinds of father-son bonding activities; moments he never had with his own father growing up.

As a child, Teddy always yearned for his father to do simple things with him. Instead, he'd only get smacked, beat or tossed around, and Felisha was no help. She was too busy shielding herself from his father's daily beatdowns, that she was unable to save her son. As a little boy, he realized that he'd never have those cherished father-son moments; he began to hate the man and wished him dead, until the opportunity presented itself, and he was able to rid the tyrant from his and his mother's life. No one ever found out, and he never regretted pushing his sperm donor down those basement steps.

He made sure he had everything he needed, then he pulled out a container of gasoline. The house that he and Monica had built from the ground up; the house that he added all his "special" effects, held a lot of secrets. Watching it go up in flames would not be such a bad idea. However, before he could finalize his plans, he had one major loose end. He needed to take care of Kyndall.

***

Kyndall splashed the water in Mark's face and tried to run to the other side of the pool.

"O, you play dirty...come here." He grabbed her by the waist from behind before she could get away.

"No, Mark, please don't dunk me in the water! I don't wanna get my hair wet." He admired the loose bun that she situated atop her head before she got in the pool. He made her a promise that her hair would be safe if she stayed in the four feet of water, but after she playfully attacked him, his promise was contingent upon how many times he could make her say "please." She tried to wiggle out of his strong grasp.

"Please, I won't do it again."

"How can I be so sure?"

"I promise," she giggled.

"Say pretty please."

"Pretty please."

"One more time."

"Pretty pretty please."

"Since you asked nicely, I'll let you slide this time." He released his hold on her, and she turned around to face him.

The sun had gone down, and they were the only two left in the pool acting like long lost friends who had finally reconnected and didn't want to part. What had started out as a tag along to ambush Devon, had turned into an all day Sunday funday—drinks, food, music, beach vibes. Mark couldn't recall the last time he had so much fun packed in one day with a vivacious, beautiful woman. Kyndall looked radiant in Monica's brand new one-piece Baywatch bathing suit. The hot pink number brought out her glowing, chocolate skin tone, and her updo allowed him to appreciate her natural beauty—slim neck, high cheek bones, almond-shaped eyes, cute nose, and luscious lips. Those lips. He was drawn to her lips. All day he wanted to kiss those lips—when she chewed her food, when she talked, when she put the wine glass against them to sip, when she licked the lingering liquid from them—he wanted to lean in and give it all he had, but he remained a gentleman and refrained from invading her space. Yet, when he saw the dreamy look in her eyes, and the closeness of her body, he was instinctively and automatically drawn in that direction. Their lips finally met.

Everything that he wished they were, they were. Her soft, thick lips were like fluffy clouds, and when her tongue searched and found his, he felt as if he was floating on one of those clouds. He brought her body closer to his, and her arms snaked around his neck. The taste of Cabernet Sauvignon on her lips and tongue had instantly become his favorite flavor. He was getting a buzz all over again. Not only was he getting intoxicated, when she ran her petite fingers down the back of his curly head, he began to get aroused. He didn't want to misread her intentions, so to save himself from getting overly excited, he gently peeled his lips away.

She slowly opened her eyes and looked into his while they held their embrace. She wiped the glistening from his lips, bit down on her bottom lip, then smiled at him. The signs were there, and what was understood, needed no explanation.

"Would you like to spend the night? I can take you home first thing in the morning."

She nodded in agreement. They exited the pool, grabbed their towels and wineglasses and made it back to the fifth floor in silent anticipation of a never-ending night.

***

Teddy rang the doorbell again, infuriated that Kyndall had not returned any of his messages or phone calls. Was she and Mark somewhere laughing behind his back? The thought of her with Mark caused hm to blank out and lose all focus. He needed answers, and he wasn't going to rest until he got them. *Where could she be?* It was getting late, and from what he knew about her, she was home by a certain time if she had to work. But then he remembered that school was out on Monday, so he wasn't sure if she actually had to work. His tunnel vision wouldn't let him think about anything else other than Kyndall. After a few seconds of waiting, Kyndall's neighbor, Rayna, stepped out the door again with a short, silk robe wrapped around her petite but busty and curvy body.

"I see you're still on the hunt for the Miss Popular Kyndall. I'm sorry to tell you she's still not home." She gave him a hungry look. He could have sworn she purred.

She saw the anger and disappointment in his eyes.

"You can wait here for her if you like. I make a mean spicy margarita."

He looked at the chocolate beauty, who was more or less offering herself up on a platter, but he already had enough complications as it was and didn't need to add to his messy life.

"Maybe some other time," he said before walking back to his truck.

"Are you sure? I can keep you company while you wait. Kyndall might not be back anytime soon, and the way that man was looking at her when he opened the car door for her, I wouldn't blame her."

Teddy's horns popped out of his head and his nostrils flared as he ignored her and kept walking to his truck. Once he got inside, he tried to call her again. No answer. He was beyond furious and curious. He started up his vehicle, then drove around the corner a few times, hoping to run into Kyndall. He figured she'd show up soon, so he strategically parked his truck on the other end of the street to await her arrival.

Monday Madness

CHAPTER TWENTY-TWO
MONDAY MADNESS

It was the top of the morning. The sun was slowly making its presence known. Miss Ruby still had not heard a peep from Yasmine. She was up all night trying to busy herself with unnecessary housework, but nothing would keep her mind off the gut feeling she had that something wasn't right. Time and time again she told Yasmine that nothing good would come of her messing around with married men. That's how her grandson, Antonio, came about; Yasmine's affair with a married man, who wanted nothing to do with his son.

Miss Ruby wanted to place all the blame on Yasmine for not making better choices, but she knew that her daughter only imitated what she saw her mother do. Miss Ruby was ashamed to admit that her poor choices in men trickled down to her daughter, and she hoped it wasn't too late to save her from those choices.

Antonio had a blast with his few friends that showed up for the sleepover and was too preoccupied to notice that Yasmine was gone, but once all the children left, he asked incessantly for his mother. Miss Ruby gave him an excuse that Yasmine took a mini vacation and would be back soon, but deep down, with the lack of communication she received from her daughter, she began to doubt her own words The conversation she had with Teddy did nothing to allay those doubts. Something about him never sat right with her. People were fooled by the handsome, fake charm, but not her. She'd seen it and lived it before. The wolf in sheep's clothing.

That was why the first thing she did when the sun began to rise was head to the police station. She walked inside and asked the officer at the desk, "Hi. Who would I speak with to file a missing person's report?"

***

Felisha stood outside her son's house ringing the doorbell.

"Where the hell is Teddy?" I told him I would drop you off this morning. He knows I go to my Monday morning step class with Sheryl. Lil Teddy, how did you lose your housekey?"

Lil Teddy shrugged while he dug inside his bookbag looking for his housekey. He knew it would appear eventually, but after dumping the contents of his bag on the ground, no luck. Felisha tried calling Teddy's phone again, but it continued to go to voicemail. An idea came to his mind.

"I can go in the back and try to open the door."

"And how do you propose to do that?" his grandmother asked, unimpressed. "I'll just have to take you back to my house until your dad shows up."

The last thing Lil Teddy wanted to do at that moment was go back to his grandma Felisha's house. It was a school holiday, and he had his heart set on eating a big bowl of Fruity Pebbles and watching his favorite cartoon, then playing video games. His grandmother only had Raisin Bran and wanted him to help her plant flowers in the garden. He hated raisins and couldn't stand gardening. He'd rather go fishing or play baseball.

He didn't want to tell his grandmother that he left his bedroom window unlocked. His father had told him numerous times not to leave it unlocked, but every time he saw a lizard climbing up his window screen, he'd open it to shoo the pesky reptile away. Before Felisha could protest, Lil Teddy ran to the backyard, unlocked the fence, pulled up a lawn chair, lifted his bedroom screen and window to get inside the house. He'd suffer the consequences of leaving his window open later.

He wanted to get his Monday plans in action. He ran to the front door and let Felisha inside.

"Young man, did you break a window or something?"

"No, ma'am." His clipped response indicated that he didn't want to answer the question, so she left it alone for the moment.

Once inside, she looked in the garage and saw that Teddy's truck was gone and the can of gasoline on the floor.

"Maybe he had a client this early," she said out loud. "Lil Teddy, you want me to fix you something to eat?"

"No, Gran. I'm going to eat cereal."

"Fine by me," she said. "I guess I'll make some coffee and wait."

***

Kyndall had her eyes closed and her head against the headrest, enjoying the short ride back home with the soft, melodic sounds of *October London* filling the small space. Periodically looking over at her and admiring everything about her, Mark couldn't help but smile. After a spontaneous Sunday filled with laughs, imbibement and good conversation, he felt that he and Kyndall had grown closer and were on the right track to establishing a solid friendship. He couldn't help replaying the pool kisses over and over in his head. He felt himself floating. *What did this woman do to me?*

When they returned to his condo after making out in the pool, they made out some more, then he allowed her privacy to take a shower. When she got out of the shower and had the plush robe wrapped around her body, Mark didn't want to rush her into anything. He gave her the spare bed to lie down on while he massaged her feet. In no time, she had dozed off to sleep. He gazed at how peaceful and angelic she seemed at that moment. It warmed his heart to have her sleeping peacefully in his home, so he decided not to disturb that peace. *When the time is right*, he told himself before he went to his own bed.

During the ride back home, with her eyes closed, Kyndall felt the magnetic energy between her and Mark. He was the perfect gentleman and had racked up a bunch of cool points by being there for her when she needed to confront Devon. In addition to that, he invited her to his home and made her feel comfortable. The kisses and the foot massage were the icing on the cake. He could have very well taken advantage of her vulnerable state and slept with her, but he was patient and made her comfortable. That spoke volumes, and he'd definitely reap the rewards at a later time. That morning, when she woke up with the comforter wrapped around her body and feeling well rested, she wondered where she was, until it all came back to her, causing her to smile from ear to ear. She had a wonderful Sunday escape and looked forward to the next time. There was definitely going to be a next time.

The sun was barely peeking out when Mark turned the corner and pulled up in Kyndall's driveway behind her car. He caressed her leg to let her know that they had arrived. She opened her eyes and lifted her head before looking over at him. They smiled at each other like they had a secret that only they shared with one another.

"So, are you going to work this morning?"

"Naw. The kids are out today. I had some paperwork to do, but I'm going to take a day off too."

"Can I call you later?"

"You most certainly can. I wouldn't have it any other way."

He got out to open her door, then stood in front of her while she got out.

"This has been awesome, although, I feel like I'm about to do the walk of shame."

"There's nothing to be ashamed about. You were the perfect lady, and I enjoyed every bit of your company."

"You're so sweet. I swear when I first met you, I thought you had this giant chip on your shoulder, and I was a bit afraid, but now I understand why." She playfully poked him in his chest. "And you sir, have been the perfect gentleman and an even better host."

He smiled and took her hands in his before leaning over to kiss her goodbye. Once again, they found themselves unable to part as their tongues did the tango, until Mark released the magnetic grip, not wanting to get overly excited upon her departure.

"Keep doing that and I'm not going to let you leave," he informed.

She smirked and ran her hand over his hard chest. "Thanks for everything, Mark. I bid you adieu until next time."

He watched her switch her hips to her front door, fiddle with her keys, and turn around and wave before she went inside her home. He had the widest grin on his face as he skipped to the driver's side and drove off, feeling like life was about to take a turn for the better.

Like a faulty pressure cooker, Teddy was about to explode. He had sat for hours waiting for Kyndall to return home, and after dozing off, he woke up to his phone ringing. His mother was calling, but he was too preoccupied with Kyndall and Mark to answer the call. Why Kyndall didn't answer any of his calls or messages became clear as he watched them with his own two eyes fawn all over one another. She'd never given him the kind of affection that she had just given Mark. He had a hard time digesting what he was witnessing. Watching her gush over Mark literally made him sick. His stomach churned, his bright skin turned red, and he felt queasy.

Mark's interest in Kyndall came as a surprise. *How could he go after her after he knew she was on my radar? Or did they already know each other and played me?* Teddy was confused and upset. He had plans for Kyndall—she was fun, beautiful, and a breath of fresh air. But now, he saw her as just another conniving, cunning cunt. Feelings of paranoia, jealousy and rage formed in his being, He felt like his world and his control were falling apart. All the women in his life—Felisha, Monica, Cynthia, Yasmine and now Kyndall—had all disappointed him within the past twenty-four hours, and he felt like a ticking time bomb.

He wanted to be the one to put that kind of smile on Kyndall's face. He wanted to be the one to make her switch her hips into the house after a long kiss goodbye. He needed to look into her eyes. He cranked up his truck and pulled up in front of her townhouse, got out, and rang her doorbell for the third time in less than twenty-four hours.

***

Lil Teddy saw his grandmother outside on the back patio drinking coffee and talking on her phone. She had her back to him, but he could tell that she was preoccupied with whomever she was talking to. He wanted another bowl of cereal, so he helped himself to some more Fruity Pebbles and rushed back to his room to watch his cartoons. He flipped through the channels while he dug up a spoonful of cereal and shoved it into his mouth. His channel surfing came to a halt when his remote died. He pressed the buttons relentlessly and shook it to bring it back to life. He told his father earlier in the week that he needed some batteries, but he couldn't recall if his father went to the store or not.

Having no luck reviving his remote, Lil Teddy figured he'd use his father's remote in the meantime. He'd used it before for his television, so he was sure it would be okay this time. The only problem was he wasn't allowed to go in his father's room without permission. He'd just run in, grab the remote, and run back out. Easy peasy. He asked himself, how much trouble could he get into?

With Felisha still on the phone outside, he dared not interrupt her. He slyly ran to Teddy's room, slowly turned the knob, and crept inside. He instantly saw the remote lying on the bed. Unbeknownst to him, in Teddy's haste to leave the house, he threw the remote on the bed, not thinking anyone would be there until he returned. Lil Teddy quickly examined the remote. It looked different than he remembered, a little smaller with less buttons, but he shrugged it off, thinking it'll work just fine, then he hightailed it out of Teddy's room before his grandmother caught him. When he got back to his room, he pressed a button, but nothing happened. He pressed a button again, then in rapid succession, he began pressing buttons, hoping something would happen.

Yasmine's sleepy eyes became alert when she heard the door opening. She was beyond exhausted from boredom and from the stress of worrying about how she was going to see the light of day again. She expected Teddy to walk through the door, but then, it shut again. Monica was sprawled across the bed, still motionless and half dead. When the door opened and closed again, there was still no Teddy. Yasmine looked up at the monitor. She didn't see Teddy in his bedroom, but she did see Lil Teddy in his room looking as if he was turning channels on his T.V. Yasmine's adrenaline started pumping. She didn't know what was going on, but she suddenly felt anxious.

The door opened slightly again; she jumped up and screamed before it closed, "Help! Get me out!" She tried to pry her body in the small crack but didn't have enough space. Monica's eyes fluttered open hearing Yasmine's cry for help.

Lil Teddy grew frustrated. His cereal was getting soggy, but he was determined to get the remote working. He opened the battery compartment, took the batteries out, blew on them, and put them back in the remote. He hit the button again. Nothing.

"Help!" he heard.

The sound gave him pause. *What was that!?*

"Oh my God! Get me out of here!!!"

His eyes grew. He peeked out his bedroom door. The cry for help startled him, and it didn't sound like his grandmother. Miss Yasmine ran past his room in a t-shirt, and he had no idea why.

"Oh my God...thank you! Get me out of this house!"

Felisha jumped up from the patio chair outside to see what the commotion was all about. "What in the world?" she said.

Felisha, Yasmine and Lil Teddy all looked at each other in shock and wonderment.

"Miss Felisha! Call the police! Call the ambulance! Where's Teddy! I gotta get outta here!"

"Chile...calm down. What's going on? How did you get in, and what do you have on?"

Yasmine was hysterical. Both Lil Teddy and Felisha were confused.

"Miss Felisha...call the police and the ambulance! Monica!"

"Monica?" Felisha asked. "What are you rambling about?"

"I need a phone! Call..."

At the mention of his mother's name, Lil Teddy's heart raced, his eyes darted between his grandmother and Yasmine. He was confused and anxious. *What's going on?* His young mind was all over the place.

Yasmine wanted to run out of the dreaded house for fear of being locked up like an animal again. She didn't see Teddy, so she guessed that he must have stepped out. Due to her recent circumstances, she didn't trust ANYONE, but she made a promise to Monica.

"Teddy's closet!" She pointed towards his bedroom.

"What about his closet? Felisha was trying to make rhyme or reason out of Yasmine's magical emergence in the house and her disheveled appearance. None of it made sense.

Lil Teddy, however, ran to his father's closet while his little heart raced. It was small, and he didn't see anything out of the norm until he saw the opening in the side of the wall next to his father's shoes, then he peered inside. The harsh lighting, the toilet, the sink...it all seemed strange to be in his father's closet. Then right there on the bed, off to the side, was his mother. She looked different, older maybe...smaller, but unmistakably, his mother.

"Mommy!" he started bawling and jumping up and down. "Mommy! Mommy!" he cried out and wept loudly, overcome with joy, sadness, bewilderment, confusion. He almost crushed her with his bodyweight as he rushed to her side and like a toddler, laid down with her on the small bed and wrapped his arms tightly around her body.

"Mommy!!!" he slobbered and bawled loudly.

Monica's heart swelled while she cried along with him as they wrapped themselves into a tight cocoon where NOBODY would be able to spread them apart ever again.

Felisha heard Lil Teddy's outburst and ran into the closet. When she saw all there was to see in the tight, hidden space, her knees buckled, and feeling faint, she fell down on them. "How? Whyyyyy?" she wailed.

In the meantime, Yasmine ran outside and banged on the neighbor's door.

"Call the police! Call the ambulance!" she demanded.

The lady looked at the hysterical woman who was dressed in only a t-shirt and knew something wasn't right.

"O my! What's going on?"

"I don't have time to explain. Can I use your phone? Call the police...NOW!"

The neighbor ran back inside, grabbed her cell phone, and dialed 9-1-1.

Time to Pay the Piper

C HAPTER TWENTY-THREE
TIME TO PAY THE PIPER

Kyndall wondered who could have been ringing her doorbell so early in the morning. "Did I leave something in Mark's car," she asked herself before opening the door. Teddy stood on the other side—eyes red, five-clock shadow, not looking himself. The look in his eyes was one that she'd never seen before. *Who is this man?*

"Teddy? What's going on? It's awfully early, and you're coming over here unannounced?" she stated in the form of a question. "That's not like you. Is everything okay?"

He didn't respond immediately. His dead stare scared Kyndall.

"Can I come in?"

"Uh...I don't know. It's early, and I have a lot of things to do. Can we talk later?"

He tried to reason with her despite his feelings otherwise. "Kyndall, I was worried. You didn't return any of my phone calls or text messages."

Her mind went to her phone that she had thrown in her purse since going to the beach with Mark. She was so in tune with her company that she cared less about her phone or who was reaching out.

"I'm sorry, Teddy. I was preoccupied and busy. I haven't even looked at my phone."

"I bet you *were* preoccupied."

"Excuse me?"

"Kyndall, I saw you."

"Saw me what?"

"Can I come in?" he asked a second time.

She had an uneasy feeling. His demeanor didn't make her feel comfortable enough to invite him inside her home. He didn't wait for an answer as he bombarded his way around her and through the threshold. She turned around partially shutting the door. He was out of order, and she was not pleased.

"Teddy, what's going on with you? This is not like you to just pop up. It's early and you're acting strange."

He turned around to face her. "I thought we had something special." He stared her down and watched her search for the right words.

"What are you getting at?"

He stepped closer to her. "I had plans for us. I thought you were special. I thought you were the one, but you're like all the rest. All you women are all the same." He kept moving closer until he was a few inches from her face. "You, Monica, Yasmine, and even my mom...you're all disappointments. And now, I'm going to ask you one more time. Why did you ignore my calls?"

Kyndall began shivering on the inside. He had her cornered and there was no escape. As diplomatically as she possible could, she said, "I went off the grid for a day to wind down."

"Interesting." He paused. "I saw you, Kyndall."

Unsure of what he was referring to, she asked again, "Saw me?"

"I saw you with Mark."

She swallowed hard.

He continued. "How could you? I bet you two had a good ol' time laughing behind my back."

"Teddy, it was nothing like that. You and I are only friends, and the same is true for Mark. I didn't plan for any of this to happen. It just did. And if I'm being honest, I'm free to see and date who I want without you questioning me." She stood firm, and then added, "Aren't you dealing with Yasmine?"

In his anger, he slapped the wall behind her, causing her to jump.

"This isn't about Yasmine! I saw you kissing Mark! You never kissed me like that. Kiss me, Kyndall." He bent down expecting her to follow his command.

She put her hand on his chest to push him back. He was immovable.

"Kiss me like you kissed him." He put his weight into her, pressing her back against the wall.

"Get away!" she yelled.

"Kiss me!"

He pressed his lips into hers. She tried to scream and push him off her.

"I thought you liked me the way I like you." He picked her up.

"Put me down! No!"

"Since you like playing with emotions, I got a lil' game we can play."

She punched him in his back. "Put me down!"

He proceeded to lay her down on the couch all while she kicked and screamed. After tossing her down, he tried to put his hands around her throat.

"You wanna play games? Let's see how long you can hold your breath before you pass out."

As soon as he wrapped his hands around her throat, he felt a metal object slam into the back of his head.

BLAM!

He felt dazed. The metal object cracked into his back.

WHOP!

"Ugh..." he groaned.

"The police are on the way. I suggest you GET OUT!"

Teddy was dazed, confused and discombobulated. Kyndall was able to squirm away from him and run to her purse to retrieve her gun while her neighbor, Rayna, stood near Teddy, ready to deliver another skull crushing blow.

"Get OUT, you creep! I knew your ass was up to no good. I could see it in your eyes."

Rayna wielded the metal baseball bat at him as he rubbed the back of his head in anger like he wanted to lunge at her, but seeing Kyndall pointing the small pistol at him, he decided otherwise. He ran out the door, hearing the sirens in the distance.

"OMG, Rayna...I owe you. I can't believe he did that. I was so scared!"

The two women embraced.

"When he came by twice, I knew I needed to keep my eyes on my camera. He didn't seem to be wrapped too tight, especially after he declined my offer for a drink. Hmmmph!"

Kyndall was shaken to the core to fully process what Rayna said. "I need to call my sister," she said while reaching into her purse to get her phone, then ignoring all the missed texts and call from Teddy.

Rayna walked to the door. "Okay. I'll be outside waiting on the police and to make sure that weirdo don't show back up."

"Kyndall!" Leila answered the phone immediately. "I've been trying to reach you."

"He...he...he attacked me." Kyndall started bawling, barely able to get the words out.

"Who?! What's going on? Where are you?"

"I'm at home. Teddy came over—"

"Teddy! Oh my God, sister! That's why I was trying to call you. Something's going on over on the other side of the cul-de-sac. Eric went to go see what all the commotion was about. The neighbor mentioned something about Teddy's house. We heard all kinds of sirens. Stay on the phone. I'm on my way!"

Still crying, Kyndall informed her sister that she needed to call Mark and let him know that Teddy was on the warpath and may be on the way to pay him a visit as well.

"Call him on the three way. I'm not letting you off the phone," Leila instructed.

Kyndall called Mark but put Leila on hold.

"Hey beautiful," he said, still on a high from their most recent departure.

"Mark! It's Teddy! He came by the house and attacked me. Apparently, he saw us outside kissing. If my neighbor hadn't come to my defense, I don't know what would've happened."

"What the hell! I'm turning around. I'm on my way back over there. I'll kill him!" he yelled, before hanging up.

He did a U-turn and headed back to Kyndall's place. After the amazing time he had with her, he didn't expect his happy bubble to burst so soon. He was intending on riding that happy wave for the rest of the day, but of course, Teddy. His phone rang a second time. Cynthia was calling.

"Mom, I can't talk now."

"Mark! It's Teddy! Something's going on over there. I'm getting in my car to find out."

"What do you mean something's going on?" Mark couldn't believe his luck. "I'm headed to Kyndall's place. Teddy attacked her."

"O no!" Cynthia couldn't believe what she heard. "I got a call from that phone you gave Lil Teddy. He was crying and I heard sirens, but the phone call disconnected, and I can't reach him back."

Mark's heart raced. He felt like he was going in circles. It was too much going on at one time, and it all centered around one person. Teddy.

"I'll meet you over there, Mom." He called Kyndall back.

She answered the phone and let him know that she was giving a report to the police while her sister was still connected on the other end.

"I need to go see if Lil Teddy is okay." He gave her the quick version of what his mother said, which wasn't much.

"By all means, please check on Lil Teddy. Once I finish talking to the police, I'm going to head over there. I'll ask my neighbor, Rayna, to ride with me."

"Okay. Be safe."

Kyndall told her sister what Mark said, and Leila agreed to go back home and wait for Kyndall and Rayna to show up.

***

Teddy rubbed the back of his head while doing eighty miles an hour to get home. The fire in his eyes was intense. All his plans had gone up in smoke. Kyndall was supposed to be the last piece of the puzzle for him and Lil Teddy to live their happily ever after.

"How could I be so stupid!" He pounded the steering wheel. "She's like all the rest!"

He wanted to go back and finish what he started. His fingers were itching to go back around her neck, as well as her neighbor's too, but at that moment, he was faced with a dilemma and a deadline. *Get Lil Teddy, burn the house down, and LEAVE!*

He looked at the time and figured Felisha should be on the way to drop Lil Teddy off. He couldn't think straight. He didn't know if Kyndall had sicced the police on him or not, and he wasn't going to hang around to find out. His quiet life was imploding, and he didn't have time to think beyond the present.

He sped home, and as soon as he turned the corner into the cul-de-sac, his heart thumped out of his chest. He came to an abrupt stop and was frozen in motion. The news crews, the ambulance, and the police were camped out in front of his house. Everything had come at him in one big swoop like a huge fishing net. All his transgressions were on display for all the world to see.

As if he was watching a movie in slow motion, he saw the EMT rolling Monica to the back of the ambulance with Lil Teddy holding his mother's hand while walking alongside the gurney with tears running down his face. He watched Cynthia jump out of her car and run top speed towards the back of the ambulance. He saw his two people on either side of his mother holding her up and leading her to a lawn chair. She was obviously distraught. He saw Eric giving his mother a bottle of water. He saw Yasmine hugging her mother, Miss Ruby, in front of the news reporter, and as soon as she saw Teddy's truck at the entrance to the street, she released her mother and screamed, "THERE HE IS! GET HIM!"

All eyes turned toward Teddy. He saw police running in his direction, so he roared the engine, but didn't have a way to get out other than to back away from the scene to try to save himself. The fireworks had been lit, and the explosion was imminent.

He began to back his truck away from the scene, and as if by design, Mark had just arrived.

"What the fuck!?" Mark said out loud as his eyes scanned the scene.

He couldn't make heads or tails of all the commotion that was going on. It couldn't have been good.

Leila had not heard back from Eric since he went to see what all the commotion was about. She was still on the phone with Kyndall while she and Rayna were enroute. According to Kyndall's last conversation with Mark, something was going on with Teddy. As soon as Kyndall and Rayna pulled up to the house, Leila immediately stepped outside and examined her sister.

"Are you okay? I can't believe he did that!" Her anger evident. "Thank you, Rayna, for being there for my sister."

"You're welcome. You know we sistas gotta stick together."

"Let's go see what's going on. Eric is in the doghouse, but he still could've let me know what's going on around there."

They all hopped in the car and drove to the other side of the cul-de-sac. When they got there, it looked like all hell had broken loose. Teddy's truck was backing up, but Mark's car was blocking him. The police were on the bullhorn telling Teddy to turn the vehicle off and exit.

"What in the world!?" Leila asked. She looked around at all the commotion at Teddy's house and saw Eric rubbing Felisha's back while an emergency medical attendant was knelt down in front of her checking her vitals.

"This can't be good," Kyndall said.

The ladies watched the action unfold.

Mark's phone rang through his car. "Mom, what's going on?"

With a shaky voice, she belted out, "Mark! Your sister is alive! We're in the ambulance! Don't let that monster get away! He had her all this time...all this tiiiiiime!"

"What!" Mark's heart swelled. His sister was alive! He needed to put his eyes on her and see for himself. His eyes teared up. But the amount of rage and hate he had for Teddy, kept him in place behind Teddy's truck. He was NOT going to let him get away.

"Step out of the vehicle!" the police shouted.

Every eye on the scene watched in quiet suspense. Nobody moved. Teddy looked in his rearview. Mark was not moving. The other car was not moving. All his hopes and dreams had just gone up in smoke. Surrender or run? He chose the latter, stomped on the gas, and turned the steering wheel to the left towards the wooded area and quickly jumped out the truck, leading the chase into the wooded trail.

He heard the police commanding him to stop. He heard the faint voice of his mother screaming his name. He heard the news reporter giving a breaking news alert. He let his long, strong legs catapult him further into the woods. He didn't know how many police officers were on his tail, but the harder he ran, the fainter their hurried steps became.

Immediately upon seeing Teddy jump from his truck, Mark got out of his car and fled in Teddy's direction. Nothing else was on his mind other than catching up to the sick bastard and unleashing his wrath. He hoped the police didn't catch up to the psycho before he did. Teddy belonged to him!

Rayna parked the car on the side of the street, and the three women hurried out the car to investigate further. Kyndall had a wide-eyed, worried look on her face. Leila hugged her, but when she saw Eric run behind Mark, she screamed.

"Eric! No!"

Mark breezed past the four, out-of-shape cops. He was hell bent on catching up to Teddy. Both Teddy and Mark were fast and determined for two different reasons. Their heartbeats hammered against their chests. One minute turned into two minutes. Mark felt himself getting winded but stopping was not an option. Lil Teddy, Monica, Cynthia, and Kyndall were his motivation. He had to right a wrong; no if's, and's, or but's about it. He was so motivated that he had gained on Teddy before he knew it, and like a tiger, pounced on the man's back.

Teddy's knees buckled, and they both tumbled to the ground. Like two beasts in the wild, the two men wanted to skin each other alive. Mark jumped up, and his fist connected with Teddy's jaw, the intensity of the blow shook Teddy. Mark wouldn't stop and showed no mercy as he kept delivering relentless and powerful punches to Teddy's pretty face. Teddy was disoriented and couldn't get his footing. He grabbed Mark's leg and pulled him off the ground. He then found a branch to help him temporarily fend off Mark and his fury. He got up from the ground and tried to hammer the branch against Mark's skull, but Mark rolled over and bounced back up. He drove his foot into Teddy's gut, bending him over, then chopped him across his spine. Teddy groaned and dropped to the ground, unable to defend himself once again against Mark. Mark repetitively slammed his foot into Teddy's face.

"You'll never hurt another woman again as long as I live! You fuckin' sick bastard!"

Eric had finally caught up to the two of them, but from what he'd learned back at Teddy's house, Mark was totally justified in his actions, so he did nothing to stop the slaughter. Teddy deserved every punch, kick, death grip or throat chop. Teddy's face was bruised and bloodied, making him barely unrecognizable. However, when Eric heard the winded cops finally approach, he pulled Mark away from Teddy, who looked like he was hanging on by a thread.

The cops could barely breathe as they came slowly one after the other, panting and trying to catch their breaths. Teddy was leaking blood and could hardly stand, but they could care less as they peeled him off the ground, handcuffed him and led him limping from the dense woods. Mark was handcuffed as well, but he didn't care. That was the only way they would be able to restrain him from actually killing Teddy with his bare hands.

By the time they resurfaced from the wooded area, Teddy's truck and Mark's car were moved; the EMT with Cynthia, Monica and Lil Teddy on board were enroute to the hospital; Felisha was still hunched over in a chair in the yard being comforted by one of the neighbors; and Yasmine and her mom were giving interviews to the news reporters.

Leila ran into Eric's arms. She gave him a temporary reprieve from the doghouse. She would hate to have had something happen to him while she was mad at him. It would have eaten her up. He bent down and kissed her. At the same time, Kyndall ran over to a handcuffed Mark and debated with the police to let him go, reasoning with them that Mark was only helping them catch that monster, Teddy. "Please, let him go."

After having a discussion with the other officers, they all agreed to release Mark. The beatdown that Teddy received was indeed justified, and without his help, Teddy may have just gotten away. They'd downplay it later in their reports.

Kyndall threw her arms around Mark, and while they embraced, she caught sight of Teddy in the back of the police cruiser with swollen eyes and a bruised face. She wanted to spit on him. She never felt that much contempt for anybody. He looked past her and saw his mother sitting in his yard crying her eyes out. She stared back at him; the heartbreak was all over her. She couldn't stop crying and shaking her head. The cruiser eventually drove off with everyone watching.

"Whew...it's early, and I didn't even have my coffee this morning, but all this drama got me on a high," Rayna said. "You think I can get an interview with the news people?" She laughed, trying to lighten the mood.

"Thank you so much, Rayna, for being there for my sister. I don't think I would be able to show just how much I appreciate you." Leila expressed her gratitude and told Eric how Rayna had come to Kyndall's rescue.

Eric couldn't believe what he'd heard. "If I'd known that, Teddy would NOT have made it out of those woods." He was incensed.

Mark rubbed his bruised hands, looked back at the house—at the police tape, at the police milling about, at Felisha who looked distraught and was still stuck in place in the front yard, at Yasmine getting her fifteen minutes of fame, at the neighbors with their camera phones out. He couldn't believe it. He needed to see his family.

"I need to hurry to the hospital," he told them all.

"We understand," Eric and Leila both informed.

"You mind if I go with you? I'll drive your car," Kyndall offered.

"I'd like that," he answered.

She hugged and thanked Rayna, who offered to take Leila and Eric back to the other side of the cul-de-sac.

After the Dust Settled

CHAPTER TWENTY-FOUR
AFTER THE DUST SETTLED

On the way to the hospital, Mark was in his own thoughts and wanted nothing more than to kill Teddy and rip him to shreds. The man didn't deserve to be breathing as far as he was concerned. Just to think that Monica had suffered at the hands of a man who was supposed to love and protect her was enough to get his blood boiling. *I should have done more to convince my sister to leave.* He partially blamed himself.

While Kyndall drove, she allowed Mark the quiet time he needed to process everything that had transpired so far. The day had started out amazingly and then it quickly turned into a circus. She still didn't know all the details but was sure all the dots would eventually connect.

They arrived at the hospital in record time, thankfully in one piece and no speeding tickets. She and Mark rushed inside the emergency room and were directed to Monica's room. Due to the delicate nature of the situation, she informed him that she'd be in the waiting room, and he promised he wouldn't keep her waiting long.

His nerves had gotten the best of him when he stood outside Monica's hospital room. His chest tightened, his heart raced and his eyes burned with unreleased tears. He slowly opened the door, and there she lay in the bed surrounded by hospital equipment, Lil Teddy and Cynthia. She looked sick and delicate. He wanted to kick himself for not being able to protect her.

Lil Teddy didn't hear him come in the room. He had his chair as close to the bed as he could possibly get with his head lying down next to Monica and his hand wrapped tightly around hers. Cynthia stood in the corner at the head of the bed gently brushing Monica's hair back with her hands. She gave Mark a reassuring smile mixed with joy and sadness, letting him know that it was okay.

"She's weak, but she's gonna be okay. Thank God!" Cynthia told him.

Mark didn't hold the tears back anymore. He couldn't.

Monica opened her eyes and weakly smiled at him, causing his emotions to erupt while he went to the other side of the bed, bent down, and held her as tightly as he could in spite of the circumstances.

"I'm sorry, sis…I'm so so sorry." He wept while she rubbed his back.

"I know, Mark. I love you so much…I know."

Even in her time of weakness, she was his strength. The four of them cried together until the nurse came into the room to check on Monica. Mark took that moment to check on Kyndall, who had been patiently waiting. When she saw him, she could tell he'd been crying, and she totally understood why. He took her hand and asked if she'd like to join him and meet his sister.

"I'm not so sure it's a good time. I know you all need this time to reconnect. I wouldn't feel comfortable imposing on your family time."

"Trust me…it's fine. I would love for you to come," he admitted.

She didn't argue, then let him lead the way. When she entered the room, Lil Teddy ran to her.

"Miss Kyndall! This is my mom!"

She hugged her little friend and saw all the emotions carved on his young face. She could only imagine the roller coaster of emotions that he was experiencing. Lil Teddy resumed his position at Monica's side like he was her personal bodyguard.

Cynthia pleasantly spoke to Kyndall and allowed Mark to do the introductions. Monica was still weak, but as soon as she saw Kyndall, she remembered her from seeing her reading and praying with Lil Teddy.

Monica opened her arms to the stranger, and Kyndall, unsure of the reception, bent down and returned the hug. Monica whispered in her ear, "Thank you so much."

Kyndall didn't know at the time, but would later find out, why Monica was so taken with her. She humored her and said, "I'm happy you're safe."

After Monica released Kyndall, she looked over at Mark and could tell that he was just as taken by Kyndall as she was. She gave him a lazy smile and uttered to him, "She's a keeper."

***

That night, after the dust had settled, Eric knew he had to come clean or his marriage would be on the rocks. By the way that Leila had been acting lately, he knew he needed to let the cat out the bag or else. While she had given him a temporary pardon from the doghouse, he convinced her to go out to dinner with him before Julian returned home from spending time with his cousins. She reluctantly agreed, but then reasoned that an evening away from the house was just what the doctor ordered after all the commotion that had taken place earlier.

The neighborhood of Calm Springs had turned into a zoo. The news outlets and the internet were abuzz with the latest headlines:

MISSING WOMAN FOUND

HUSBAND HID HIS WIFE

MISSING FOR TWO YEARS WOMAN FOUND ALIVE IN HER OWN HOME

HUSBAND KIDNAPPED WIFE AND MISTRESS

In less than one day, Teddy's face was plastered everywhere, and the captions and memes went viral.

Eric decided to take his wife to a restaurant near the marina where they could sit outside with an exquisite view of the lake. He still felt bad about missing out on the wonderful dinner and backyard picnic she had planned and executed. He knew in due time he'd have to recreate that same picnic in the near future. In the meantime, he needed to lay everything out on the table.

After they were seated by the hostess, Leila couldn't hide her delight at the beauty of their surroundings. The lake offered a serene setting for the patrons to dine, light jazz music played in the background, the evening sky was clear, and the temperature was perfect for outside dining. They ordered a couple of cocktails, and while waiting, Eric took his wife's hands and expressed his deep sorrow for not returning home at his usual time, even though he didn't intentionally or actually do anything wrong. He ate his pride to make sure she was satisfied.

Since the failed picnic and all the Teddy drama, Leila had softened her heart towards her husband and her marriage. She couldn't imagine the torture that Teddy's wife went through. He was definitely not the man they thought he was. She looked at Eric and was reminded of how awesome he was and how she had definitely lucked up when the stars aligned and they met.

She was getting ready to tell him that all was forgiven until she saw the hostess pointing a woman in their direction. Leila's smile faded when the caramel-colored, petite woman was laser focused in their direction She was pretty and had a certain aura of class around her. Her short hair was secured with finger waves that perfectly framed her face and she wore a cream linen pantsuit with straps on the shoulders. Her matching beige heels gave her a little more height. Eric turned around to see what had caught his wife's attention, and he immediately stood up to greet the woman as soon as she approached the table.

"Hi Eric," she said, going in for a hug.

"Anastasia," he said, being polite and giving her a quick hug back.

When her lipsticked lips happened to accidentally meet Eric's collar, Leila was instantly in fight mode. That was the same color lipstick that she saw on his shirt in the dirty laundry. She was getting ready to stand up and act a fool until he introduced her.

"Anastasia, this is my lovely wife, Leila."

With a wide smile, Anastasia greeted her. "Hi, Leila. I've heard so much about you. I hope I'm not interrupting, but your husband insisted that I come."

"Oh, he did?" Leila gave them both the evil eye.

"Anastasia, have a seat." He pulled out a chair for her.

Leila felt herself getting hot and couldn't believe the audacity of both of them. "What is this about?" she angrily asked.

Eric waved his hands in surrender. "Baby, before you get riled up. I know you've been wondering why I've been a bit elusive lately, and I see this going down the wrong road. So before it gets out of hand, I wanted to come clean."

"Come clean? Eric?"

Anastasia felt uncomfortable. She could see Leila's temper rising, and she didn't want to be in the middle of the married couple's disagreement.

He sighed. "Leila, you made it impossible for me to sneak behind your back, so I just want you to know what I've been up to, and with that being said, I want you to know one thing..."

Leila held her breath. She was on the verge of ransacking the whole restaurant.

"...you ruined the surprise, but..."

All smiles, Anastasia pulled a small folder from her purse and laid it on the table in front of Leila. The folder was decorated with Anastasia's logo, AW, in a fancy font, along with a picture of a Caribbean background.

"AW? Anastasia Worldwide." Leila started to connect the dots. "Ohhhhh...you're AW?"

Eric answered, "Yes. She's the travel agent I've been working with to try to put together a surprise birthday escape for you. I wasn't too sure how to go about it myself, so your sister recommended Anastasia."

Leila felt stupid. She palmed her face and shook her head, then perused the contents of the folder that contained an itinerary for a week-long birthday trip to the Maldives, a place she always told her husband she wanted to go. Eric had gone all out to get her the perfect gift, and she had the nerve to be suspicious of his behavior. She then became emotional, and the waterworks began.

"I'm sorry, Eric. I didn't mean to ruin your surprise. My behavior was uncalled for." She sniffed. "I can't tell you how much this means to me and how much YOU mean to me. I should have never doubted you."

He took her hands into his and reassured her with a gentle smile.

"Well, lovers...if my job is done, I told my husband to meet me here at the bar."

Leila looked at her. "I feel so foolish," she giggled. "Thank you for helping my husband. It's the best gift ever."

Eric stood. "Thanks for everything, Anastasia. We'll tell you how the trip goes."

"Please do and send me pics for my website and social media."

"Certainly will."

After Anastasia walked off, Leila couldn't hide her embarrassment. "I owe you an apology. Kyndall tried to tell me to stop trippin', but I was convinced you were being shady behind my back."

"I know. She told me, and I knew I needed to put your mind at ease. The last thing I ever want my beautiful wife to think is that I'm being unfaithful. It's only you, Leila. It's always been you, and it'll forever be you."

She got misty eyed. "Did I tell you how much I love you?"

"Not today, but I know."

"You're the best husband a woman could ever have, and tonight I'll show you better than I can tell you."

"And I look forward to it."

They clinked their glasses and drank their chosen cocktail

"Wait...did you say that Kyndall told you about my suspicions?"

Eric laughed. "Drink up, dear."

A New Beginning

CHAPTER TWENTY-FIVE
A NEW BEGINNING

FOUR MONTHS LATER

"Happy birthday to you! Happy birthday to you...." They all sang in soulful harmony as Leila walked out to a host of family and friends who stood around the beautifully decorated table that sat along the beach with miles of the beautiful turquoise ocean as its backdrop. Leila was gorgeous in her beach-inspired, tropical-colored, spaghetti-strapped dress with long curly hair that framed her face. Her bare, pedicured feet with neon pink toes stepped in the soft sand as she walked out to her birthday fanfare with her arm tucked inside Eric's. He complemented her well in his blue raspberry colored shorts and lighter blue short-sleeve shirt that accentuated his muscular physique. He too with a fresh pedicure minus the polish that he and his wife had done earlier as a couple's package.

Leila's parents, Julian, Kyndall, Mark, Cynthia, Lil Teddy, Eric's brother and wife, and even Monica were all in attendance. When Eric planned his wife's birthday trip to the Maldives, he never expected the extra addition of family and friends, but he was happy they all jumped on board to help celebrate his wife's special day, as well as enjoy the beautiful island. It was breathtaking—the overwater villa with private pool, lounge deck, the outdoor shower, the marina, the tiki bar, the bedroom that offered a full view of the ocean and the blue sky, and other priceless amenities. He knew it wasn't going to be easy to leave the island behind when it was time to go. In the meantime, he'd take full advantage of the amenities that the resort had to offer.

Just as breathtaking as the island was, his wife was equally and even more breathtaking. Eric saw the never-ending joy on her face since they'd arrived on the island a day ago. He was pleased that he and Kyndall were able to secure a good package deal with Anastasia. He chuckled to himself when he thought back to Kyndall and Leila's playful argument about Kyndall being in cahoots with Eric and not telling her about Anastasia. Leila argued that her sister could have saved her from stressing over Eric's behavior, but it all worked out in the end. In Kyndall's words, "That man hasn't looked at another woman since he laid eyes on you." He had to agree; Leila was his everything, and she deserved nothing but the best.

"Happy birthday, Leila!!!!"

"Woohoo!"

"Thank you...everyone." Leila thought her face was going to crack from the permanent smile that had been etched on her face for the past two days nonstop.

She made her way around the table and hugged her parents. When they learned of Eric's plans to visit the Maldives, the retired beach hippies immediately made plans to attend. Spending time with both their daughters and their grandson, Julian, was an added bonus to indulging in the incredible island. They'd already made plans to stay an extra two weeks and island hop. Leila's birthday was just the excuse they needed to try a new getaway.

Leila then hugged her sister and best friend, Kyndall, who was glowing and seemed to be the happiest that Leila had ever seen her. She knew without a doubt that Mark played a huge part in her happy disposition.

"Your chocolate skin looks like it's been kissed by the sun," Leila laughed in her ear.

"The sun's not the only thing that's been doing the kissing." Kyndall grinned and looked over at Mark.

He winked at her. Ever since their Sunday Funday, they'd been joined at the hip. Kyndall had played an integral part in helping Monica get acclimated back to her new life and had become a welcome addition to their family. Two months before their trip to the Maldives, Mark treated Kyndall to a second Sunday Funday. After bar hopping along the coast, they had once again ended up at Mark's condo. Red wine, good conversation, and kisses in the pool not only led to another foot massage but a night that neither one of them would ever forget. The new lovers took their time exploring one another and found their happy place in each other's arms.

Mark never thought it was possible to fall head over heels so quickly, but he was convinced that that's what happened because every minute of the day, she was on his mind—from sunup to sundown. Their Sunday Funday turned into a weekly ritual, and Kyndall was just as hooked on Mark as he was on her. The foundation was laid, and they were steadily building and fortifying their relationship.

Mark was the next person to receive a hug from the birthday girl. She was glad that he was only sentenced to community service and had to pay restitution to the bowling alley. Ultimately, he was cleared to travel overseas and accompany Kyndall to the island. His helping the police apprehend Teddy worked in his favor. He was looked at as the town hero. Leila was proud to have him amongst their family and friends. Ever since Eric had given Mark and Kyndall's friendship the stamp of approval, she knew that he would be the man for her sister. They not only looked aesthetically pleasing, but she could tell they were mentally and spiritually in sync.

He was a protector, a provider, and a loving family man, and Leila knew without a doubt that Mark would be the man that her sister would meet at the altar. He checked all the boxes, and she couldn't wait to put on her matron of honor dress when the time came, and according to the secret ring-shopping conversation she overheard between Eric and Mark, the time was not too far away. She giggled to herself. She would happily keep that information to herself for the time being.

When Leila made her way around the table to hug Cynthia, she was truly ecstatic that she was able to come. Not only was she invaluable with helping with the boys, but the women and their families had developed an unbreakable bond by way of Mark, Kyndall and Lil Teddy. After two years of tragic loss—losing her husband while Monica was missing—Cynthia stayed strong and prayed and it paid off. She was in a happy place. Her children were back together, and her life with her grandson had resumed. Leila admired the woman's strength and faith. The four women—Cynthia, Leila, Kyndall and Monica—began going on self-care dates to the spa and to luncheons to laugh, talk, cry and overall let their hair down, mainly for the sake of Monica's well-being. The quartet had become a thing in a short period of time, and in the near future, she was going to be proud to call them all family.

Julian, standing beside Lil Teddy, couldn't wait to hug his beautiful mom. She bent down and gave both the boys a tight squeeze. Her son was blossoming into a handsome and younger version of his father—caring, considerate, generous, and all the things she would hope that he'd be. He was an amazing friend to Lil Teddy and assisted as best he could to help Lil Teddy conquer his sadness surrounding Teddy's misdeeds and incarceration, although Lil Teddy had a whole village rallying around him. The two boys had become inseparable, along with Yasmine's son, Antonio. They were the latest version of the Three Amigos, but one was currently not able to join his buddies on their island getaway because he was enjoying himself in California, Disneyland to be exact.

During Yasmine's fifteen minutes of fame after she was seen on the news giving her account of being one of Teddy's hostages, she became social media famous, and all the men were drawn to the green-eyed damsel in distress. Teddy's long white t-shirt and her messy hair did little to detract from her outward beauty. Her DM's were flooded with offers of marriage, trips, cars, shopping sprees, and the like, but ultimately, it was one handsome suitor and independent wealthy jeweler, Jay McMillan, who won out. Not only was he rich, but he was also single, and after seeing the green-eyed beauty, he was instantly smitten. He not only wined and dined her, he made sure Miss Ruby and Antonio were included in the plans he had for Yasmine.

Jay McMillan had whisked them all away to California for the week, and Yasmine was loving every minute of it. She was finally dating someone who only had eyes for her and vice versa. She was ashamed of the way she acted with Teddy and the person she allowed herself to become. Making good on the promises she made to Monica while they were trapped together, she initiated establishing a non-profit organization for battered spouses. She and Monica were in the pre-planning stages but was proud to spearhead a worthwhile cause. She would never look back and become that desperate Yasmine ever again. For her, it was way more rewarding to love and have that love reciprocated in the right way, and Jay was the right person for the job.

When Leila finally made it to the last person to receive a hug, she spread her arms out wide and embraced the woman the hardest and the longest. Monica was a true survivor and a strong woman who had endured a horrific experience and was able to rise above to reclaim her life that Teddy had stolen from her. What he had done to his wife was unimaginable, and it made Leila realize that she should never again judge a book by its cover. They all thought that Teddy was a genuinely good person and an outstanding father and never once did they question his character. Boy, had they been fooled.

Monica mentally received the hug from Leila and felt truly blessed for her new family of friends, Mark's new romance, Lil Teddy's resilience, and a new outlook on life altogether. That first month of being thrust back into the world was an adjustment period for her. She had to get her physical health back on track, the weight was coming back, and she even trained with one of the female trainers at Eric's gym.

Her mental health, however, was more of a challenge. She no longer cared to be in confined spaces or behind closed doors. Harsh fluorescent lights were triggering; her PTSD was at an all-time high. Not only did she have to adjust to her new normal, but she also had to come to terms with her father's death. Not once had Teddy revealed to her that her precious father had passed away from a grieving heart. That revelation took a lot out of her. She spent the first month crying, praying, and holding onto Lil Teddy and Cynthia. Lil Teddy never left her side. He was stuck to her like glue, and she knew the mental trauma that he experienced as well. They were all getting family counseling. Being a counselor herself, Kyndall would also act as friend and therapist whenever needed. Monica adored Kyndall from the moment she laid eyes on her in Lil Teddy's room reading the book with him. Mark had indeed lucked up and won a prize.

Monica was thankful for her mother, brother and son. Collectively, they were definitely her rock. Would she ever trust another man ever again? She couldn't answer that question, but she did know that she couldn't let Teddy win and leave her miserable for the rest of her life. Before catching the flight to the island, she was able to convince her family that she needed a face-to-face with Teddy, the monster, himself. Eric's brother, who worked at the jail, was able to finagle her a quick visit with Teddy.

When Cynthia sat down behind the glass and watched Teddy be ushered out to her like the criminal that he was, she felt vindicated. She also felt pity looking at the man that she used to love with every fiber in her being. She could honestly say that she never really knew him at all, and that she was in love with the idea of him. She could tell that he had been in a fight or maybe two because he was bruised and battered and looked like he'd seen better days. That was of no consequence to her, though, because he had brought it upon himself and deserved every beatdown he received. She waited for him to pick up the phone, then she did not hesitate to let him know how she felt.

"You wanna know what's so funny?" She said, staring straight at him. "You did all that to me just to take me away from my son, and now, who is the joke on? Ironic, huh? You're a cruel, hateful monster. You traumatized me, you traumatized your son, AND your mother. I hope you rot in that little ass cell just like you wanted me to rot. The two years of torture I en-

dured will be nothing like the lifelong torture you'll experience just knowing that your son is out here living and thriving with his mother and NOT with you!"

Teddy's face turned red. She could see that her words affected him.

"And that beautiful woman, Kyndall...she and Mark sure make a gorgeous couple. And guess what else?" she continued to taunt him like all the times he would taunt her. "I heard through the grapevine that he's getting ready to propose to her. I can't wait to see the pretty babies they're going to make."

Teddy kept quiet, but he couldn't hide the inferno that was going off inside his body.

"O yea...and Yasmine...remember her? We're actually becoming good friends and are going to start a non-profit together. Hmm...go figure. Guess you were good for something after all. Inspiration. She's actually doing pretty good for herself these days...got her a rich man who adores her AND he's single."

"And let me not forget Lil Teddy. My beautiful, darling son. He's gonna be NOTHING like his daddy. Me, Mark, my mom, and even Kyndall will see to that!"

Teddy gritted his teeth and banged on the window with his fist as hard as he could. He couldn't take anymore and wanted to get to the other side and tear Monica to shreds. How dare she? He thought.

The guards immediately restrained him as Monica watched as she gave him the last laugh before she walked out of the dank jail and into the sunshine.

"Everybody, this is the BEST birthday I've ever had, and that's because of you all! And also my handsome and delectable husband who put this thing together." she grabbed Eric's hand. "This island is everything! And I'm happy to share my day with all of you." She raised her glass and asked all the adults to raise theirs as well. "TO US!" she cheered.

"TO US!" They all replied before downing their beverage of choice.

Leila's birthday celebration lasted well into the night as they all danced, laughed, drank, ate, and told tales until one by one everyone eventually retreated to their respective villas and put a cap on a wonderful day.

***

Felisha had one last errand before she caught her flight to Italy. She looked forward to a new start and a new life to escape the shame and embarrassment of what her son had done. She loved Lil Teddy with all her heart, but she knew her presence in his life at the moment would be too much for the both of them. She needed to get away and never look back. Teddy had broken her heart, and his confession that he was the reason that her husband hit the bottom of those stairs, let her know that her son was damaged a long time ago, and she was oblivious to it. She promised to never go back to visit him behind those bars. It was too much to bear.

The "for sale" sign sat in front of the house like it was any ordinary house on the block. It was not. It represented all the things that were wrong with her son. Who could raise a family in that home with all that bad energy?

She used the garage door opener that she got from Teddy's truck and went inside before letting the garage back down. She picked up the gasoline can that was still on the garage floor and walked to the dreaded dungeon that her disturbed son had carved out inside his closet. She doused the small prison with the strong fuel and went throughout the house repeating the process in each room.

She eventually lit a match that started the domino effect of crumbling down the house, then she exited as if nothing happened. By the time the firefighters would get to the house and put out the flames, it would be in ruins, and she'd be long gone.

With a cracked heart and a tear-stained face, Felisha started her car and drove away just as quietly as she came, promising never to return.

THE END

Miz B says:

An author is a chef of words, characters, emotions and plots, who stirs them all together to come up with a dish in the form of a story that he hopes will please the literary palates of those who partake in the journey.

Thanks for allowing me the opportunity to take you on that journey. I hope it was worth it.

I love it here!

Follow me on Instagram: @mizbthewriter

For book discussions, join the group on FB: Miz B's Fun Reads

www.ingramcontent.com/pod-product-compliance
Lightning Source LLC
Chambersburg PA
CBHW060324310726
48976CB00007B/2437